"You're Not A Cowboy, Michael!"

Dusty yelled. "If you've suddenly decided to become one, don't ask me for a job. Me, of all people."

She had honestly thought the hurt wouldn't surface, that it was buried so deeply it would never sting again. But she was feeling all of the pain. How could Michael just stand there and pretend he hadn't inflicted a wound that might never heal? No apologies, not even a hint as to why he'd gone off without a word.

Maybe he'd forgotten the whole episode. Maybe he had just thought of Wyoming, remembering somewhere along the line that he knew a cattle rancher.

But now she was hurt, embarrassed and terribly humiliated. Never in a million years could she have imagined him showing up like this. She'd tried to forget him and their marriage sixteen years ago, and now here he was, bringing all those memories back....

Dear Reader,

Happy New Year! And what a *fabulous* year it's going to be. First, due to *overwhelming* popular demand, we have another fun-filled lineup of *Man of the Month* books... starting with *Lyon's Cub* by Joan Hohl. In the future, look for *Man of the Month* stories by some of your favorite authors, including Diana Palmer, Ann Major, Annette Broadrick and Dixie Browning.

But Silhouette Desire is not only just *Man of the Month,* because each and every month we bring you six sensuous, scintillating, love stories by six terrific writers. In January, we have Jackie Merritt, Amanda Stevens (this is her long-awaited sequel to *Love is a Stranger* and it's called *Angels Don't Cry*), Kelly Jamison, Cathie Linz and Shawna Delacorte.

And in February we're presenting a special promotion just in time for Valentine's Day called *Mystery Mates.* Read and see how each Bachelorette opens the door to love and meets the Bachelor of her dreams. This promotion is so wonderful, we decided to give you six portraits of the heroes, so you can see each man up close and *very* personal.

Believe it or not, that's just what I have in store for you the first *two months* of 1993—there's so much more to come! So keep reading, enjoying and letting me know how you feel.

All the best,

Lucia Macro
Senior Editor

JACKIE MERRITT

A MAN LIKE MICHAEL

SILHOUETTE *Desire*®
Published by Silhouette Books New York
America's Publisher of Contemporary Romance

SILHOUETTE BOOKS
300 East 42nd St., New York, N.Y. 10017

A MAN LIKE MICHAEL

ISBN: 0-373-05757-1

First Silhouette Books printing January 1993

Printed in the U.S.A.

JACKIE MERRITT

and her husband live just outside of Las Vegas, Nevada. An accountant for many years, Jackie has happily traded numbers for words. Next to family, books are her greatest joy, both for reading and writing.

One

———

Dusty Tremayne believed that she understood men as well as a woman could. Understanding herself, however, was quite a different matter. She did foolish things with men, for men, *because* of men, or she had in the past. Two unsuccessful marriages and several near misses was not a record that Dusty was proud of. In fact, it scared the living daylights out of her. She was weak where men were concerned, very strong otherwise, but let a good-looking guy with a sexy, crooked grin give her the eye and she got all giddy and overheated.

She had vowed, *vowed*, to never let it happen again. Handsome, well-built men could parade around in G-strings, she adamantly told herself, and she would not react.

Dusty had taken a trip, left the Tremayne ranch in Wyoming and gone to Florida for two weeks. She couldn't bring herself to call it a vacation, not when it was time she needed to recover from the rather dramatic demise of her most recent—and final, she swore—relationship. The trip was not meant to be fun, and she wasn't looking for excitement. Rather, she planned to do a lot of soul-searching.

First of all, the idea of being unmarried, or at least unconnected for the rest of her life, was extremely disturbing. So was having no children. She loved her friends' kids and wanted babies of her own. She was thirty-three years old and had been batting zero on that score, so her decision to live without the opposite sex was unquestionably traumatic.

But she couldn't seem to ever find the right guy, the mate that not only filled her own needs but was also good father material. Men were such cads, she'd come to feel, smiling and sweet and loving until they got a woman right where they wanted her. Then how the worm turned! Trent, her second husband, had actually resented a simple "I love you" after a few months, as if her saying those lovely words was some kind of unreasonable demand on his emotions.

In all fairness, Dusty's first marriage hardly counted. At seventeen she and her boyfriend, also seventeen, had eloped. They had been tracked down and brought home, and an annulment had been arranged. The episode was a distant memory for Dusty, as she had never seen the boy again. He had been spending the summer on a ranch about fifteen miles from the Tremayne spread, but his time in Wyoming had come to a screeching halt by his and Dusty's big romance.

Her second marriage had been for real, though. Or so she had thought. Trent had proved himself to be a complete rounder, with a roving eye and a penchant for spending money, both his and hers. The other men in her past added up, each one going off with a piece of her heart. With every episode, her own self-doubt got bigger and more pronounced. Why was she so different from her friends? Not that every one of them had a perfect relationship. But they'd all done a lot better than she had.

Maybe it boiled down to something as simple as bad judgment, Dusty mused. Maybe she was lacking in the necessary traits to make sound assessments of the men she met. Or maybe her hormones were a little too active. When she was in love with a man, she wanted to make love with him. She wanted to talk about love and bask in romance. Was that attitude abnormal?

She was really very confused about herself, Dusty admitted again while walking along the beach, kicking up sand with her bare feet. She was not promiscuous, she reminded herself, glad of that positive aspect of her personality. The men in her past were people she'd known, not pickups or one-night stands. It was just that there were a few more than there should have been, and she was feeling a bit bruised from her most recent failure.

She was walking with her head down, barely aware of the spectacular beauty of the beach and the lazy, rhythmic breaking of the Gulf waters against the pale sand, or of the lush greenery surrounding the variety of houses paralleling the shore. Dusty was staying in one of those houses, one of the smaller units that were rented out to snowbirds during the winter season.

Dusty looked taller than she was, mainly because of her long legs and firm, almost-boyish hips. Any curves Dusty Tremayne had were centered in one specific section of her trim body—her bosom. Her arms were slender, her shoulders rather wide and squared off. Today she was wearing a one-piece white bathing suit and a large black straw hat, under which she had tucked her straight, shoulder-length, honey-blond hair. Dark sunglasses concealed a good portion of her face, and she had tied a fringed black-and-white shawl around her waist, devising a cover-up so she wouldn't be doing her beach pacing in only a bathing suit.

Seeking emotional comfort, Dusty added up what she considered a few more of her good points. She was not an exhibitionist; her modest bathing suit was proof of that. She was not a flirt; men sought her out, not the other way around. Her goals of a good solid marriage and children seemed perfectly normal. Her IQ was high, she wasn't afraid of hard work, and she never expected something for nothing.

Dusty sighed. She could list her good points from now until kingdom come, but the fact remained that she had a dismal history of failures with men. She was definitely doing something wrong.

Was she too friendly? Too trusting? Too romantic? She believed that stardust and moonbeams should remain in a relationship, and they never did.

No more mistakes, she told herself. No more falling in love and being disappointed. No more unnecessary hurts. The next time a man came on to her, he was going to be thoroughly dissected before he got so much as a smile out of her.

She had turned over a new leaf, and she was determined to follow its strict parameters.

Mrs. Cora Potter, dressed in a softly flowing, lavender morning gown, topped off Michael Crowley's coffee cup with a gracious smile. "I do so appreciate your taking time from your busy schedule to visit me, Michael."

"My pleasure, Cora."

The elderly woman smiled again, a teasing twinkle in her blue-gray eyes. "Leaving New York at this time of year probably wasn't too much of a hardship."

"It was forty degrees and drizzling rain when I boarded the plane," Michael said with a pointed glance at the sun-drenched beach. They were breakfasting on the terrace of Cora's winter home near Sarasota, and Michael's bones were gratefully soaking up the warmth.

"And how is your father?"

Michael had arrived the night before, but the hour had been late and Cora had merely shown him to his room, stating that they could talk in the morning. He'd gotten a good night's sleep and was mentally prepared to work on the new will Cora thought she needed.

"Working too hard, as usual," Michael replied.

Cora Potter had been a valued client of the Crowley law firm and a good friend of the Crowley family for many years. Her husband, too, until his death four years before. "Some people don't know how to relax, Michael."

"Yes, but Dad's been warned by his doctor."

Cora drank from her coffee cup. "George was a lot like that. Smoked those awful cigars until the day he died, no matter how many warnings his doctor issued." Cora chuckled softly. "He lived eighty-two reasonably happy years, so I can hardly judge his habits, can I?" She set down her cup. "And your brother and his family?"

"They're fine. Tom and Dad are cut from the same cloth."

Cora smiled fondly. "Yes, they are. And what about you? How are you doing?"

Michael looked away. "I'm all right."

"You look all right but I sense something amiss. You're not...content. Is that the right word?"

Michael brought his vivid blue eyes back to his hostess. "Is it that obvious?"

Cora was eighty-one and a lady who minced few words. "Remember that I knew you when you were very content, Michael. What's wrong? Aren't you getting over Lisa's death?"

Michael got up and walked over to the terrace railing. He shoved his hands into his pants pockets and looked at the beach scene. He was tall and dark-haired, a handsome man of thirty-three. He had a flair with clothes and looked trim and neat in pale cream slacks and a casual, ivory linen shirt.

"It's been almost two years," he said quietly. "I should be over it, don't you think?"

"We all handle grief differently, my friend."

He laughed cynically. "That's the problem. I'm not handling it at all."

"You've faced your loss, haven't you?"

"I know she's gone, yes. I know my wife was killed by a hit-and-run driver, I know I'm alone. There's a lot more to it, though, Cora. A whole lot more." Michael took a long breath. "Nothing's the same. I don't...enjoy anything anymore."

"Your work?"

"Drives me up the wall."

"But you always loved the law."

"Idealistic babble, Cora." Michael turned, leaning his hips against the rail. "May I talk to you about something?"

"Of course."

Frowning, Michael looked away from the sprightly little woman for a moment, then back to her. "I've been thinking about giving it up." If he'd surprised Cora, she hid it well. "I'm tired of the rat race," he added grimly.

"Well . . . is there something else you would rather be doing? Another career?"

"There's the bind. I know what I don't want, but I have no idea what I do want."

Cora smiled. "You're a young man and have plenty of time. I'm sure something will occur to you. Would you like some more coffee?"

Sighing inwardly, Michael returned to the table. As good a friend as Cora Potter was, he was here in her home on business, and he shouldn't be laying his problems on her. "I'll have a little more, thanks."

Cora filled their cups. "Do you like it here, Michael?"

"It's a beautiful place."

"Why don't you stay a few days? Unless there's some reason you need to rush right back to New York, of course."

"That's a nice invitation, Cora. Let me think about it." A few days in the sun? Yes, he could stand a little more sunshine, and a telephone call to New York would rearrange his schedule without too many hitches.

And there had always been something tranquilizing about Cora, maybe because of her good taste and refinement, which Michael had been noticing, as usual. Her home, whichever one she might be using, was elegant without being too formal. Her table was always set nicely and generously, and guests were treated as if their presence was important to her.

Cora Potter was truly a lady, Michael thought, a lady in the grand tradition, and he was feeling more at peace in her company than he had in a long time. Was this what he was looking for, a quiet, elegant life-style such as Cora's?

He finished off his coffee, no closer to an answer than he'd been, although he felt pretty certain that he wasn't looking for "quiet and elegant" as a permanent condition. This was a pleasant interlude, but the unknown goal he was searching for had to have substance, solidity.

"Let me know when you're ready to discuss the terms of your new will, Cora."

"I have a few things to attend to this morning. Perhaps after lunch?"

"Whenever is convenient for you."

Cora neatly folded her napkin and laid it beside her plate. "Why don't you change into something less restricting and take a nice walk on the beach? It's such a lovely morning, much too pleasant to be cooped up inside."

Michael scanned the beach again. There were a few people strolling along the water's edge, a few others who were taking the sun at a more energetic pace. Sunlight reflected off the water in dancing beams. Gulls swooped and screeched. A dog ran past, followed by a boy of about eight. A light, warm breeze ruffled Michael's hair.

How long had it been since he'd aimlessly wandered a beach? Walked barefoot in sand?

Michael's gaze narrowed on a woman walking alone. A tall, slender woman in white and black. She was too far away to see clearly, but he perceived a strong sense of her femaleness. An internal ripple of awareness surprised him, something primal and almost forgotten, an involuntary response of his hormones to a woman's. In the next heartbeat he felt a stirring of something familiar and frowned at the sensation. Logic made acquaintanceship unlikely, but there was something about her...

"A lovely view," Cora said softly.

"Pardon?" Michael tore his gaze from the beach and the mystery woman. "Oh. Yes, it's a . . . great view."

"You really must consider staying beyond today, Michael. We could get our business out of the way this afternoon and then you could relax and do absolutely nothing until you tire of it."

"That might take a while."

"However long it takes, I would be pleased to have you as a houseguest. Perhaps a break in your ordinary routine would give you a more distinct perspective." Cora leaned across the table and took her younger friend's hand. "I've lived a long time, Michael, and if anything breaks my heart, it's seeing someone with so much potential for happiness letting it slip away. If you're truly discontent with your life, do something about it."

"Did you? Ever?"

Cora sat back and smiled. "Ah, that's a very long story, my friend. Let's not squander this beautiful day in old tales."

"But I would like to hear it."

"Then you shall. But not this morning." Cora pushed herself to her feet. Michael got up and came around the table to offer his arm, which Cora took. "Now," she said as they left the terrace and entered the house, "you go and enjoy yourself. Lunch will be served at twelve-thirty, then we shall get our legal discussion over and done with."

"Whatever you say."

After Cora had gone off to another part of the house, Michael slowly climbed the stairs to his room. He hadn't planned on mentioning his personal dissatisfaction to Cora, nor had he thought of extending his short business trip beyond what was necessary.

But maybe this opportunity shouldn't be passed up. Sorting things out in his own home wasn't working. Too many memories, probably. If nothing else, he should sell the condo and find another place to live.

Michael shook his head. It wasn't just the condo, nor was it "just" any one other thing. It was a combination of remembered happiness and tragedy, and of somewhere along the line losing any resiliency to snap back that he might have once had. It was New York and his career and his friends and yes, his family.

Closing the door of his room behind him, Michael went to the mirror and looked himself in the eye. Guilt was the toughest part of his indecision, guilt because he knew he had it good, a successful law career, enough money, his health. He said low and accusingly, "You're a mess, Crowley, a damned mess."

He'd brought along a jogging outfit—shorts, a T-shirt and a pair of athletic shoes, which would have to do for that walk Cora had insisted he take. He hadn't jogged this morning as he'd tentatively planned, anyway, and a little exercise would feel good.

He changed clothes.

Dusty noticed the boy and his dog. They were an exuberant pair, running, playing, cutting up. The boy had an infectious laugh, and Dusty found herself smiling, as though she were part of his games. Untying the shawl from her waist, she spread it on the sand and sat down to watch.

The boy was a rugged little fellow, dressed in long, baggy tan shorts and an oversize blue-and-red T-shirt. A baseball cap was turned backward on his head, so that the bill hugged his nape. The dog was big and black and shaggy, and his bark was deep and cavernous, a mixed breed that would give a prowler second thoughts. The animal was so full of fun, however, he was practically twisting himself inside out to please the boy.

Yards and yards away a man jogged past, and Dusty took a moment away from the boy and dog to admire the jogger's splendid physique and long, muscular legs. Obviously he was not a native, not with that pale skin.

Her own pale skin was taking on a golden glow from her three days in the sun. She tanned easily, and Dusty knew that by the time she returned home, she would be practically mahogany, even with protective sun block.

She sighed. A perfect tan really wasn't very important, not without a man to admire it. Her gaze lingered on the jogger. Marvelous hair, longish, springy-looking, a rich, dark color. Broad shoulders. Very trim waistline.

Why, he looked like . . .

Going back in time, Dusty became very still. The jogger reminded her of Michael, the boy she had deemed herself so in love with at seventeen that elopement had seemed sensible. Her heartbeat quickened at memories that she realized now were both wonderful and disturbing. If they had been older, if they'd been further along with their education, their love would have been applauded rather than censured by their families.

She'd been forced to accept the annulment. For a while the Tremayne household had been in an uproar. Michael had been whisked back to New York, and she had never received so much as a postcard from him. Her letters to his New York address had received no replies, and her telephone calls had been intercepted. She had tried to contact him through the family he'd been staying with in Wyoming, but everyone concerned had put up a solid wall of defense.

Their love had been good . . . and so very innocent. She hadn't known how innocent until years later.

Dusty gave herself a quick mental shake. Was this any way to cure herself of almost-fatal romanticism?

She deliberately turned her head so the jogger was out of range. She was disappointed to see that the boy and dog had run farther down the beach.

Rising, she shook the sand from the shawl, retied it around her waist and started walking again, this time heading for the house she had rented for two weeks.

Michael turned back, fully intending to get another look at the woman. He slowed down when he saw her walking in the opposite direction. What he'd wanted to do when he realized she was sitting on the sand was to go right up to her and ask point-blank to see her face and hair. Jogging past her, he'd really only caught sight of the curve of her cheek below her dark glasses and wide-brimmed hat, but that one glimpse had nudged memory. He was far from positive, but he was having some very strange suspicions about her identity.

She was diagonally traversing the width of the beach, heading for the houses. But which house?

Michael's hunch was growing stronger the longer he looked at her, and he kept track of the woman's progress while he walked. She approached a small, white, stuccoed house four away from Cora's. Most of the homes were stuccoed, most were white. The color variations ranged from flamingo pink to pale gray. Some were large and sprawling, like Cora's, and some were small, like the woman's.

She disappeared inside, and Michael slowly passed the house, giving it a thorough inspection. It, too, had a terrace overlooking the beach, one that contained a bright blue umbrella table and redwood patio furniture. He saw no sign of anyone else, no man, no children.

Michael felt driven to pursue his hunch, but he had to ask himself why. The woman wasn't likely to be Dusty Tremayne, but if—by some crazy twist of fate—she was, what would he do about it? What possible reason was there for him and Dusty to meet again?

He kept on walking and pondering the matter, but he couldn't deny an odd excitement. Dusty was long in the past, a sixteen-year-old memory.

But some part of him hadn't completely forgotten her, and that portion of Michael Crowley, perhaps merely the remnants of his adolescence, was suddenly alive and demanding recognition.

The house was arranged so that the bedroom and the living room had a view of the beach. Dusty thought it was a nice little place, and had been enjoying her stay as far as accommodations went. She had stocked the kitchen on her first day from a nearby market, as she wanted to prepare most of her meals. Dusty had no desire to play tourist. She'd come for a rest, a break in routine and some heavy-duty thinking. Besides, she had been to the Sarasota area before and had taken in the sights on that trip.

Actually, Dusty tried to get away from Wyoming for a few weeks every winter. January always seemed interminable to her, and by February she was ready for a change of scene. Afterward, she was always glad to go home to the ranch. She was very lucky to be able to leave at all, she knew, and if it wasn't for the trustworthy couple, Luke and Nancy Wilkens, who lived with her in the main ranch house, she wouldn't be able to go off the way she did. Luke was her right hand with the ranch, and Nancy took care of the house. It was a good relationship, and Dusty valued it.

Deciding on a shower, Dusty shed her bathing suit in the bedroom and started for the bathroom. The window glass was tinted, allowing one to see out without anyone seeing into the house. For some reason she glanced at the beach, and she stopped in her tracks when she spotted the good-looking jogger she'd admired earlier.

He was looking directly at her house. Dusty's pulse sped up. There was no mistake, the man was walking along slowly and giving her house a detailed inspection.

She stared and admitted again his similarity to the Michael Crowley she remembered. He was quite a distance away, so she couldn't make out details of his features. He was heavier, more filled out than the young man in her memory. At seventeen, Michael had been thin. This man was not thin, but his body had an appealing leanness.

She swallowed what seemed to be a nostalgic lump in her throat. Her heart was fluttering. He couldn't be Michael. That sort of coincidence didn't happen in real life. What she was feeling, darn it, was sexual response to a handsome man, and this one was particularly dangerous because they hadn't even gotten a really good look at each other and he was making her feel things she shouldn't be feeling. Things she had been vowing *not* to feel.

Groaning, Dusty scrambled for the bathroom and jerked on the shower lever. Before the water temperature had time to warm up, she stepped beneath the spray, shocking her traitorous system with the cold blast. How could she make such ardent promises to herself one minute and react to a man she didn't even know the next?

Cora had a companion living in her home. The lady, Mary Tanaka, was of Japanese descent, around sixty years of age, and the person who kept Cora's household in apple-pie order. Unquestionably Mary was more friend than paid servant to Cora, but she was a woman of great tact and politely declined an invitation to join Cora and Michael for lunch. "You have business to discuss," she said in her soft, faintly accented voice.

Michael noted that Cora did not object to Mary's refusal, so he offered no comment on the matter. They took their seats in the dining room, and Mary served.

"Did you enjoy your walk?" Cora asked.

"Very much."

"Have you decided in favor of staying?"

Michael smiled. "Yes, and I owe you a thank-you for the invitation."

Cora looked pleased. "I thought you might stay if you gave it a little thought, and you owe me nothing. After lunch we will get our business out of the way. I want you to relax."

"You're a very special lady, Cora."

She laughed. "A busybody?"

"Never that."

A few moments of silent enjoyment of the good food went by. Michael looked up from his plate. "Do you know your neighbors, Cora?"

"Some of them. The local population has changed a great deal in the past few years. Plus," Cora added with a smile, "you must remember that at my age, one's circle of acquaintances keeps getting smaller." She held up a hand at Michael's remorseful look. "I didn't say that to raise your sympathies. I've lived a full life, and I'm not sitting around lamenting its passing."

"I know you're not."

"Was there someone in the neighborhood you wished to meet? Mary knows a few people that I don't. Some of the homes are rented out during the season, you know. When George and I built here, there were enormous distances between homes. Gradually everything filled up."

"Progress," Michael commented dryly.

Cora laughed. "Yes, progress. Was there someone..."

"No. I was...merely wondering." Michael felt a little silly for even introducing the subject. Did he really want to meet a new woman? That was all it would amount to, should he pursue the matter. Since leaving the beach, he'd consciously tried to convince himself that the mystery woman couldn't possibly be Dusty, and then asked himself if he wanted the burden of a new relationship.

That was what seemed so destructive about his increasingly dissatisfied mood. Everything felt burdensome, in one way or another.

When they were finished at the table, Cora brought her guest to a small parlor. She offered Michael a seat at a rather feminine desk and settled herself on the sofa. "Now, let's get this legal mumbo jumbo out of the way so you can enjoy your vacation," she said firmly.

Two

Each sunlit day in Florida seemed more perfect to Dusty than the one before. She was seated at the table on her terrace, eating a breakfast of melon, toast and coffee. She'd closed the umbrella over the table, as the morning air was perfect without shading.

It was early and few people were on the beach. Dusty had brought a book out with her, but it lay on the table beside her plate. Instead of reading while she ate, as she'd thought she might, she scanned the beach and absorbed the view. Blue water, even bluer sky, a few very high, fluffy white clouds. Lovely.

Her system suddenly went on alert: Yesterday's jogger was back, loping along at a steady pace.

Dusty looked at the man, took a sip of coffee and looked again. She could caution her hormones to behave until she turned old and gray, but no woman with even partial eyesight could miss that guy, and her vision was twenty-twenty.

But looking didn't necessitate anything else, she told herself. One could look and admire without going even one small step further. What would she do, anyway, chase the guy down the beach? That wasn't her style. There was some pride connected to the fact that she didn't chase men. Any and all chasing in her past had been from the opposite sex; she'd been the target, granted, probably too often, but not because she'd knowingly issued invitations.

Attitudes regarding personal relationships could be confounding. She had women friends who actively and openly chased after men, women who approved of and applauded a freer morality for their gender. One, in particular, had a favorite speech: *Men have been doing it for centuries, why not women? What does a guy do when he gets horny? He finds himself a woman, right? Well, what's wrong with women doing the same thing with men?*

Dusty couldn't quite swallow that argument for promiscuity. And her attitude had nothing to do with social diseases, or worse, although nowadays a person had better think twice before jumping into bed with a stranger. But her morality was all mixed up with emotion. She had never made love with a man she hadn't been *in* love with; her problem was that she fell in love too easily.

It was not going to happen again. Even if the guy had the power to weaken her knees from a long way off, like that jogger did. *And* strongly resembled Michael Crowley, the first major love of her life.

Dusty continued watching the man's progress on the beach, and her gaze narrowed as she wondered if he would still remind her of Michael up close. Yesterday she'd gotten only a brief look when he'd jogged past, not nearly enough to clarify that point.

Oddly enough, she started thinking about intelligence, which she truly appreciated in a man. Although, in her experience, most men were pretty adept at covering up any lack thereof. The male ego covered up an enormous amount of flaws, for that matter. Some men were terrific with bravado, and when they were hot on the trail of a woman they could be charming and witty and just plain adorable.

It was later, when the flames started cooling, that a man's true nature emerged. *And* his IQ.

If she ever met a man with wit, charm, looks, sex appeal *and* intelligence, she might reconsider her personal policy against aggressive behavior.

The thought brought a smile to Dusty's lips.

Well, it wasn't apt to happen today, she thought, getting to her feet and gathering up her plate and coffee cup. She stopped then, noticing that the jogger had turned around. He could have gone on down the beach for miles, but he seemed to prefer jogging in this vicinity.

What's more, he wasn't staying near the water. Dusty stared. He wasn't really coming this way, was he?

She was wearing plain white shorts and a baggy white shirt, which were adequate but not particularly becoming. Her face was completely devoid of makeup, her hair barely brushed.

She had to forcibly stop herself from running into the house and doing something silly, like slapping on a little makeup.

Michael had spotted the mystery lady on her terrace, and at the sight of her blond hair he'd actually stumbled. Its color was exactly as he remembered Dusty's! His legs—despite yesterday's vacillation—had immediately started taking him in her direction. He had to find out who she was, and the closer he got, the more suspicious he became.

Still, it was like a blow to the belly to realize that she *was* Dusty!

Breathing hard from his run, he stopped right in front of her terrace. "Good morning."

Dusty put down the plate and cup and stepped closer to the railing. She felt incapable of speech, for she was looking directly into Michael Crowley's blue eyes. Michael...after sixteen years. He was more mature, but he still looked very close to the image she carried in her mind.

Breathlessness threatened, while her heart began beating a mile a minute. This wasn't possible. She was in Florida, a thousand miles from New York, farther than that from

Wyoming. How had this happened? What was he doing here?

Michael tried grinning and didn't succeed very well. "Don't you remember me, Dusty?"

"Michael." Her voice sounded almost creaky, barely above a whisper.

They were both struck a trifle dumb. Being in the same place at the same time was unbelievable after so many years.

Michael cleared his throat. "I saw you yesterday, on the beach."

"I saw you, too, but I . . . didn't recognize you." Dusty lifted a slightly trembling hand to her hair. "I did and I didn't. You looked familiar, but I couldn't believe . . ."

"I know what you mean. This is incredible." Michael was beginning to think again. "How are you?"

Dusty's system was suddenly weighted by a strange wariness. Michael's good looks were unnerving. "Um . . . I'm fine. You?"

"Fine, too. I'm visiting. Four houses down. Is this your house?"

"It's a rental."

"Do you still live in Wyoming?"

"Yes, same place."

The discomfort between them was thick enough to slice. Striving for normalcy, Michael let his gaze sweep the beach. "Beautiful spot."

"I like it." Michael had been running without a shirt, and Dusty was trying not to notice that his skin was glistening like the morning dew.

"Is this your first visit to Florida?" he questioned.

"No, I was here one other time."

"Are you here alone?"

The question gave Dusty a funny feeling. Did she want Michael knowing anything about her?

She said a rather reluctant, "Yes."

Michael frowned. Dusty wasn't very receptive. Ordinarily he didn't need to be kicked in the teeth before taking a hint, but it had been so long since he'd been interested in a woman. Interested in anything, for that matter.

"Maybe we could talk," he said.

Dusty just looked at him. They had a past, the two of them. They had actually stood before a justice of the peace and sworn to love and honor each other until death parted them. Instead their families had done the parting, which was neither here nor there at this late date. But they had shared kisses and dreams and made plans, unrealistic as they'd been. Sixteen years had gone by and she didn't know this older Michael, nor was she sure that she wanted to know him. One mistake per man was enough, wasn't it?

"Michael...I don't know."

He heard the ongoing reluctance in her voice, but couldn't stop himself from attempting persuasion. "No harm in a little conversation, Dusty."

It was a crazy situation, one that Dusty couldn't have imagined in a hundred years. Michael wasn't any more comfortable than she was, but he wanted to talk.

She honestly didn't know how to say no to such an innocuous request, but she wasn't eager to agree, either. What she needed, she realized, was some time to absorb the shock of running into Michael, to figure out the odd feelings banging around in her system.

They stood there, Michael on the ground, Dusty on the terrace. "You look wonderful," Michael said. "Exactly the same."

She smiled doubtfully and became even more wary over what sounded like a line. Everyone changed in sixteen years. Proof of her changes were depicted in her photo albums.

"Could we have lunch together?" Michael asked. "Or dinner? Anything, Dusty, you name it."

Rudeness was not a normal part of Dusty's makeup, and with Michael so hopeful, she simply could not tell him a flat-out no. Besides, he was probably right about conversation causing little harm. She was just so stunned by this bizarre turn of events.

"Come by this evening, if you'd like."

He nodded. "Thanks, I'll do that." To Dusty's intense relief, he began backing away from the terrace. "Don't see sunshine like this in New York at this time of year."

"No," she agreed quietly. "I'm sure you don't."

"See you this evening."

Smiling weakly, Dusty watched him turn and start running, involuntarily taking note of the smooth, fluid way his muscles functioned.

Slowly, with her legs strangely rubbery, she sank onto one of the redwood chairs. Michael Crowley—my God. She watched him jogging down the beach and still could hardly believe the past few minutes.

Her decision to steer clear of men didn't seem appropriate to Michael's intrusion. This was not like meeting someone new and wondering if he had something against commitment, or if he maintained standards that conflicted with hers, or even if maybe he was the man she had always hoped to run into. This guy was Michael, her first husband, albeit for only a few hours a very long time ago.

Dusty stared at the beach and registered very little beyond the diminishing figure of Michael as he got farther away. She had loved him at seventeen, been totally thunderstruck by her first adult feelings for a man.

But they'd gone only so far with kissing and petting. Saving themselves for their wedding night, they'd called on their restraint. She should have practiced such remarkable restraint in later years, Dusty thought ruefully, thinking of her second husband, who'd wooed her into bed before their wedding ceremony, and a few other guys whom she wished weren't part of her past.

Pondering innocence, Dusty got up and put her hands on the railing. Her first love. There was something very startling about that fact, and that he was here in Florida at precisely the same time she was. Questions began bombarding her: Who was he visiting? Was he married? Did he have children?

She was remembering things now. Michael's father had been a lawyer. There'd been some mention of a family law firm. Was Michael a lawyer, too?

Sighing, Dusty left the rail, picked up the plate and cup again and went inside. She certainly did not need another romance, and at this point, did she even need Michael's friendship?

Dusty puttered away the day, strolling on the beach, making a call to the ranch to check in with Nancy and Luke, and trying to read. She failed at the reading because it wasn't possible to concentrate on fiction with Michael in her thoughts.

He was, most likely, the best-looking man she'd ever seen, for what that was worth. For years, she recalled, she had measured every male she met against Michael, but gradually that ritual had faded away. It was possible, given the shocking reminder she'd received today, that she might renew that old habit. One did not easily forget a man who looked like Michael did, whether he was seventeen or thirty-three.

She didn't trust herself. Her vows to remain cool around attractive men didn't seem to relate to Michael, maybe because she'd been thinking in terms of strangers. She and Michael didn't know each other anymore, but they weren't strangers.

If he suggested another meeting after this evening, would she refuse? Her pulse reacted to the idea. After sixteen years, Michael still affected her.

Dusty was stretched out on the chaise longue on her terrace, having placed the chair so her legs would be in the sun and her face wouldn't.

There was a lot more to this new-leaf program than she'd foreseen. Was she going to lead a celibate life just because the perfect man didn't come along? *Could* she lead a celibate life?

She had a lot to think about. Unless she was rationalizing away her former staunch position because Michael had appeared on the scene.

Dusty sat up, moving quickly, startled by her own thoughts. She did not want another false relationship and that was final. Funny, though, that she was thinking so hard about relationships and celibacy when Michael only wanted to talk.

Sighing, Dusty lay back again. What did Michael want to talk about? After so long, what did they have to discuss? Her life was in Wyoming; his was apparently still in New York.

They were worlds apart, in more ways than mere miles.

Michael did some shopping that afternoon. Laden with packages containing new slacks, shirts, beachwear and underwear, he returned to the Potter house to find Cora and Mary absent. A note conveyed a message of an appointment with Cora's optometrist.

He couldn't get Dusty out of his mind. Since speaking to her, he'd thought of little else but seeing her this evening. His curiosity about her was so overpowering, he repeatedly cautioned himself against presenting too many questions. She'd been stunned, as he'd been, that much was clear. How she might perceive this strange turn, once the shock wore off, could only be guessed at.

What remained surprising for Michael was how important their accidental meeting seemed to be. The evening ahead loomed as some sort of high point in his life. True, he knew very little about Dusty. His knowledge of her was years old and only so distinct. But he felt alive again, and logic wasn't very influencing against physical euphoria.

He'd called New York yesterday afternoon, but he forced himself to dial his office number again, as he'd told Blythe, his secretary, that he would call in at least once a day.

Blythe reported that everything was going smoothly and he was not to worry. "I've delayed this week's appointments until further notice."

"I won't be here more than another day or two, Blythe."
Michael wondered about what he'd just said. How long was
Dusty planning to stay in Florida?

"Don't rush it. You haven't had a vacation in a long
time."

They discussed a few of Michael's cases, which Blythe
had continued to work on in his absence, with Michael giving her some instructions she requested.

Then Michael asked if his father was in the office. He
wanted to pass on a hello from Cora. "No," said Blythe.
"He didn't come in today."

"Anything wrong?"

"Not that I've been told."

"Is Tom there?"

"Tom's in court today."

"Oh, yes, the Lawson-Sykes case. He has Cora's number, Blythe. Leave a message on his desk that I called.
Dad's, too. And make sure this number is available to anyone else who might need it." The firm employed four other
attorneys, two paralegals and numerous secretaries.

"I'll do that."

Michael put the phone down thoughtfully. It was a rare
day when his father didn't show up at the office.

But then, it was just as rare for Michael not to be there.

After a light supper of tuna salad and iced tea, Dusty took
her book out to the terrace. The sun was going down and she
wouldn't be able to read for long, but the book was becoming more of a prop than anything else, anyway.

She thought of Michael. Her own life was more dramatic
than the plot she'd been attempting to follow. Within the
past ten years, she had lost both parents, inherited the Tremayne family ranch in Wyoming, and been married and divorced. Getting her bearings with the ranch and then
ultimately operating it successfully, with the able assistance
of Luke and Nancy Wilkens, had been interspersed with the
rise and fall of several personal relationships.

Dusty had always marveled when she heard women commenting on the shortage of available men. There'd never been a shortage in her experience, quite the contrary. This holiday was a perfect example. Michael had popped up out of nowhere, making her wonder again why she was destined to meet so many men when she only wanted to meet the "right" man.

Michael wasn't him. The right man for her would be a rancher, someone who was as irrevocably tied to Wyoming as she was. That's where her heart lay, Dusty knew. She loved the ranch she'd grown up on, loved horses and the immense blue sky and the prairie and the mountains. She was a country girl and always would be. Her annual excursions to a warmer climate took nothing away from her ingrained affection for her home. Rather, they bolstered her need for the wide open spaces, and she always returned to the ranch rejuvenated and ready to tackle the numerous projects forever awaiting attention.

Holding the book on her lap, Dusty's gaze lingered on the panorama of sea and sky. The sun was setting in a pink and orange sky, a glorious sight. She had showered just before supper and was wearing a comfortable caftanlike garment, made out of a pale pink, heavy gauze fabric. Moments like this were rare on the ranch. There was always something that needed doing, always someone around. This sort of tranquility was hard to come by in Dusty's everyday life, and she planned to enjoy it while she could.

She felt calmer than she had earlier. If Michael really did drop in, she would be able to deal with it. He only wanted to talk, and why shouldn't they talk? They hadn't only been romantically involved that summer, they'd been friends.

Incidents trickled through her mind. Dates consisting of horseback rides or driving to Casper to see a movie, evenings of merely driving around the countryside and talking.

Their first kiss. Their dawning awareness that their feelings were important. It was with her again, all the time they'd spent together. The laughter they'd shared, the special moments. She hadn't felt at all immature, she recalled. Nor had Michael seemed as young as he'd been.

That summer had been the happiest of her life, which seemed inordinately sad now.

"Hello, Dusty."

Dusty's head jerked around. Michael was looking over the side rail of the terrace; he must have approached the house from the street instead of the beach. "Hello," she said evenly, although she noticed that her heartbeat suddenly seemed erratic.

"Isn't that sunset something?"

"Spectacular," Dusty murmured.

"Reading?"

He was looking at the book on her lap. Dusty closed it and set it on the table at her right. "It's a little too dark to read." She had an inner battle to contend with. Tremaynes did not mistreat visitors. Her natural tendency toward cordiality was gnawingly insistent, and she had told Michael it would be all right for him to come by this evening.

She felt tense, but kept it out of her voice. "Would you like to come up on the terrace?"

"Yes, thanks." Michael rounded the corner of the terrace to its three steps.

Dusty sucked in a sharp breath. Michael looked fabulous in cream-colored slacks and shirt, glowingly handsome. She sat up straighter and gestured to a patio chair. "Sit down, if you'd like."

"Thanks." Michael took the chair.

Dusty felt his gaze and turned her head to look at him. There was color in his face because of the sun he'd been getting. His eyes were as blue as sapphires and regarding her with undoubtable admiration. He smiled. "This is like something out of a movie, Dusty. The second I saw you on the beach yesterday, I was hit by recognition."

"When you were jogging."

"Before that. I was having breakfast on my friend's terrace. You were walking near the water. I think that's what struck me as familiar, your walk. I really didn't know for sure until today, when I saw your hair.'' Michael gave a short laugh. ''To be honest, I wasn't altogether positive until I came closer.''

''Are you an attorney?''

''Yes.''

''Here on business?''

''I came on business, but I stayed for the sunshine.''

Michael scooted his chair around so he could see her better. ''Dusty, are you married?''

Her mouth felt dry. ''I was. I'm divorced. Do you specialize?''

''Corporate law, mostly.''

Their conversation wasn't connecting. Neither of them was at ease. Abruptly Dusty got up. ''Let me get you something to drink. I have soft drinks and iced tea.''

No liquor in the house was surprising to Michael. Not that he preferred alcohol, but Dusty looked very sophisticated and he could easily visualize her offering a guest a martini. ''Tea, thanks.''

He watched the subtly feminine movements of her flowing garment as she went into the house. A pleasing scent lingered in her wake. She was an exciting woman, beautiful. He'd told her she hadn't changed, but she had. He could see the differences now, the more mature planes of her face, the adult qualities in her voice and actions.

She came out with two glasses. Michael stood up, and she passed one to him without eye contact. His eyes narrowed slightly, because her evasion seemed deliberate.

Why he was here on her terrace wasn't clear to him. Why he'd pressed her into this evening raised some questions in his own mind.

But he wasn't sorry he had. He had barely noticed that other women were females since his marriage four years ago, and certainly hadn't been interested since Lisa's death. He was interested now, and it seemed nothing short of miraculous that the recipient of that interest was a woman he'd been married to for a few almost-forgotten hours sixteen years ago.

He sat down when Dusty did. "Oh, look," she exclaimed, indicating the beach. Michael saw the boy and his dog, and smiled. "He's a great little guy," Dusty said. "There's an older man with him this evening. I'll bet he's the boy's grandfather."

"You like kids."

Dusty shrugged. "They're hard not to like."

"Do you have any children?"

"No." Dusty turned her head to fix Michael with a direct look. "Do you?"

Michael shook his head. "Afraid not. I'm a widower, Dusty. I lost my wife two years ago."

Something painful hit Dusty, and her rigid expression relented. "I'm sorry." Their gazes held, with Dusty nearly melting from compassion. "I'm very sorry," she repeated in a voice that had become husky with emotion. She had an almost irrepressible desire to console Michael, but she was also thinking that he had married again and so had she. Their lives had truly taken separate paths, and that seemed sad when she remembered how earnest they'd been that summer, how positive that neither could live without the other.

Michael spoke softly. "It's good seeing you again."

It was good seeing him again. Maybe too good. A disconcerting roar began in Dusty's brain. Where was this heading? She'd been burned enough, maybe all her own doing when she rushed into relationships pell-mell. She'd vowed to think the next time, but the "next time" seemed to be upon her, and was she thinking clearly?

How did a woman think clearly with a racing pulse and an urgency within her own body? There was something very strong and influencing between her and Michael, and if it was only temporary again, heaven help her. She didn't want to spend the rest of her life going from man to man. She wanted one solid, irrevocable relationship, one loving, lovable man. Only one.

Hoping he might be Michael would be futile. He lived in New York City. His career was there, his memories, his family, his *life!* Everything she was and could ever be was in Wyoming.

Besides, she was putting the cart before the horse. Compassion and a racing pulse did not constitute a relationship, particularly in this screwball situation.

Michael's voice remained soft. "Seeing you again has knocked me for a loop. We were only kids when we got married, but..."

Dusty let out a sound that was somewhere between a nervous hiccup and a cough. "I think it would be best if we forgot that summer, Michael."

"I'm not sure I can. Dusty, I'd like to see you, take you somewhere, spend some time with you."

The people on the beach were becoming obscure in the gathering darkness. The terrace was shadowed. Michael's voice was raising goose bumps on Dusty's skin. She was afraid, she realized, afraid of doing something she would later regret. And she would regret it if she returned to Wyoming with another heartbreaking memory.

This didn't seem real. The last time they'd been together had ended badly. They'd been embarrassed to have a group of shocked adults—her family, the people Michael had been staying with—swoop down upon them and condemn them for foolishness. If they hadn't been so positive they were doing nothing wrong by getting married, they would have covered their tracks, gone farther from home. As it was, they'd been easily found.

What astounded Dusty was how touched she was by seeing Michael again. Not nostalgically. This was not like running into an old friend that she hadn't seen in years, although it fit that category, too. But her inner self was so affected, so disrupted, and she couldn't get involved in another short-term relationship, she just couldn't. "Seeing" Michael would only cause problems.

"Michael," she said quietly. "Let me be frank. I've made some mistakes...with men...and I don't want another one. I don't know how to say it any plainer."

"I don't think we'd be a mistake."

"We were a mistake before and we would be again."

"What makes you think so?"

"Because of distance, if nothing else." Dusty winced. That sounded like she would be expecting a great deal out of any association at all if they didn't live so far from each other! "I'm not explaining myself very well."

"Something like this doesn't happen every day, not to me, at least. All I'm asking for is a chance to get to know you. For you to know me."

Dusty looked at him. "To what purpose, Michael?"

Michael formed an uneasy smile. "You get right to the point, don't you?"

"You're not used to an outspoken woman, apparently," Dusty observed. "Michael, I was always outspoken, even sixteen years ago. You must remember that."

"You were great. I can't pretend that I've spent the past sixteen years thinking about you, but that doesn't mean I forgot what happened that summer."

"I haven't forgotten, either, but we should keep it in a sensible perspective."

"What do you consider sensible, Dusty?"

The question was presented gently, but it jolted through Dusty. She dampened her suddenly dry lips and spoke in an odd, hoarse voice. "We're talking, but it shouldn't go any further."

"That's your brain speaking. What does your heart tell you?" Michael leaned over the arm of his chair, wishing he was seated close enough to touch her. "Dusty, this isn't trivial to me."

She coughed out a strange laugh. "We've barely met again, and you've already decided it isn't trivial?"

He sat back. "You don't believe me."

"I don't believe you know. How could you?"

"Dusty, something happened when I saw you, maybe nothing more than memory. But we meant a lot to each other before, and we weren't ready to be separated the way we were."

Michael stood up and set his glass on the table. "I'd like to see you tomorrow. I'll be on the beach early. Please join me."

Dusty rose slowly. "I . . . don't know."

"I can't force you."

"No."

"But I'm asking." Michael moved closer to her, lifted a hand and touched her hair. He rubbed a strand between his thumb and forefinger. "It feels the way I remember, soft and silky. I guess it's up to you."

Her own heartbeat was choking her. "I guess it is."

He bent down and pressed his lips to hers, and she closed her eyes and allowed the brief, bone-jarring contact. "You don't play completely fair, do you?" she whispered when he raised his head.

"I always thought I did." He tried to see into her eyes in the dim light. "Good night. I'll see you tomorrow morning."

Dusty stood there while he left the terrace and disappeared around the side of the house. Her entire system felt out of sync, her head pounding, her heart pounding.

Just because a man had barely kissed her? *Come on, Tremayne!*

But it was true. She was breathless and achy because of a simple kiss.

You could have pushed him away! You could have gotten all huffy and let him know he was presuming much too much!

Suddenly disgusted with herself, Dusty flounced into the house, remembered her book on the table and flounced back outside to get it.

Everything had gotten very quiet. She stopped and looked at the nearly deserted beach, and a tremendous loneliness came out of nowhere and struck her painfully hard. Dusty endured it for a few self-pitying moments, then shook off the feeling and went back inside.

She locked the door securely and closed the drapes.

Three

Dusty put in a long and restless night. Three times she got up and wandered the dark house, each time forcing herself back to bed and praying for some uninterrupted sleep.

Michael Crowley—after all these years. She felt internally shattered and outwardly fragile, a sensation she had never experienced to such an alarming degree.

It seemed miserably unlucky that the first test of her more sensible attitude toward men should come from Michael. At one point during the night she stared through the kitchen window at a high moon and wondered if she shouldn't evade the whole thing by going home in the morning.

But leaving wasn't what she wanted to do. What she wanted was... Dusty bit her lip. Her own body kept reminding her that she was a woman with a healthy sexual appetite, and she was having a hard time keeping erotic fantasies at bay, every one of them focused on Michael.

They had not consummated their brief marriage; they had never made love. She should not be putting Michael and lovemaking in the same thought now, but the chemistry that had drawn them together sixteen years ago seemed to be every bit as potent today. The major difference between them then and now was that their youthful innocence of that halcyon summer was glaringly absent.

An affair was all it could be between them. Her time here was limited, and she had no idea how long Michael was planning to stay.

An affair with the man she was once married to. How— the word kept popping into her mind—*bizarre*.

By dawn she felt thickheaded, as though her brain was wrapped in cotton. Glad the night was over, Dusty dragged herself to the shower and stood beneath a cool spray until her head had cleared. She dried off slowly, mulling it all over again.

Dusty's conclusions were a bit different this morning. Her battle, she realized, was personal, a one-on-one war with herself. Michael was not to blame for her present attitude; neither could she blame any other man who happened to find her attractive in the future. She had made an emotional decision, she now felt. She was not a woman to live without a man, and attempting to force herself into that mold would result in unmanageable stress.

She would see Michael again, she had to. She felt something for him, from him, that she couldn't simply wish away. There was one possibility that seemed like a safety valve to Dusty: Spending time with a man sometimes resulted in every speck of affection draining away, and she knew relatively nothing about Michael's habits. Some practices turned Dusty off completely—vulgarity, for one. Drinking to the point of nausea for onlookers was another bugaboo, or even a hint that the guy was stupid enough to fool around with drugs. She honestly didn't believe that Michael was inclined to any such traits, but there were other turnoffs, like blatant inconsideration, or being an opinionated know-it-all.

What she was hoping for, Dusty finally admitted, looking herself in the eye in the bathroom mirror, was that a little time with Michael would cure her of any and all nonsensical feelings for him.

If it didn't...

Leery of that conjecture, Dusty concentrated on her appearance. She fixed her hair, applied makeup and dressed in white shorts, a blue T-shirt and a pair of canvas shoes. Then she went to the kitchen, put on a pot of coffee to brew and opened the drapes across the slider to the terrace.

Michael hadn't slept well. He'd awakened repeatedly to ponder the odds of two people meeting again after so many years. It would be less incredible if he'd gone to Wyoming, or even if Dusty had been in New York. But Florida?

He thought about her reluctance and if she would join him this morning, as he'd asked. It seemed so crucial, monumentally important.

What was he feeling for Dusty? It wasn't ordinary, he knew, but he hesitated to label the urgency in his system.

Michael was walking along the shore, going slowly, not even slightly concerned about jogging this morning, although he was dressed for it. He kept looking at Dusty's house, willing her to come through her terrace door and down to the beach. His hope was tinged with anxiety, because if she didn't come out, he would have to knock on her door. He'd never thought so much about destiny, but something had brought him and Dusty to this particular spot on the globe at the same time.

Sixteen-year-old memories were upon him this morning: Dusty on horseback, her hair shining in the sun; Dusty in the moonlight, with her lips wet and swollen from their kisses; Dusty standing beside him, her hand in his, while they exchanged marriage vows.

Then later, the two of them in the small motel they'd chosen for their wedding night. The door bursting open. The disapproving anger of her parents, the recriminations of the couple he'd been staying with. He'd never been so attacked before, and judging by Dusty's face, neither had she. Stunned, they'd meekly given in to the harsh directives of their elders. He'd been brought straight from the motel to the airport in Casper and put on the first plane going east.

The trip had been a nightmare, taken up with self-accusations of cowardice and a dozen imagined scenarios where he made a much better showing, where he stood up to Dusty's parents and defended himself and his wife.

God, he'd been young. Seventeen wasn't even dry behind the ears. A boy. A kid. And he'd asked Dusty to marry him.

Michael smiled wryly. He'd had brass, if no real courage.

His father had met the plane. Michael had been rebellious, resentful, but John Crowley was not easily shaken or influenced by a pouting face. His teenaged son had made a bad mistake, which would be corrected, and that was that.

Michael had tried calling Dusty, to no avail. His letters weren't answered and he didn't know if she got them or not. If she wrote or phoned, it was kept from him.

Time passed and so did his anger. College was interesting and he made a lot of new friends. Then there was law school, and finally, going to work at the Crowley law firm. Along the way there'd been girlfriends, but no one special until Lisa.

One time, shortly after he met Lisa, Michael was going through some old things that had been stored in a cardboard box in the attic. There, in his hand, was a snapshot of Dusty. He sat down, suddenly weakened by memory, and studied the picture. For the first time he realized what a truly beautiful young woman she'd been at seventeen. Small wonder he'd been so smitten.

He thought about calling her, just to say hello. Just to find out how she was.

He never made that call. He'd had a date with Lisa to get ready for, and he'd put the snapshot back into the box and his memories back into the past.

Like he'd told Dusty, he hadn't spent the past sixteen years thinking about her. But fate, or something, had brought them together again, and at a particularly low point in his life, to boot, which in itself seemed meaningful. Add to that the fact that his emotions were greatly affected by Dusty. For the first time in ages he felt excited, charged up, even eager. Kissing her last night had been impulsive, and the sensation of her warm soft mouth against his had probably contributed to his restive night.

He knew one thing for sure: He wasn't going to walk away from Dusty like he'd done the first time, meekly and against his will. He wasn't trying to predict anything for the two of them, but he was driven to explore what he was feeling and to see where this strange twist of fate might lead.

When Dusty did come out on the terrace, Michael stopped dead in his tracks with an almost melting pleasure. She had the startling ability, even at a distance, to shock his senses. She could deny till doomsday what he'd said about this not being trivial, but it wasn't. Not for him.

She waved and he waved back. Then she made a beckoning motion with her hand. He began walking in her direction, relieved that she at least intended speaking to him this morning.

She looked beautiful in white and blue, as fresh as the morning itself. "Hi," he called when he was close enough.

"Good morning." Dusty waited for him to approach the steps. "Would you like to have breakfast with me?"

The invitation surprised and pleased him. Michael put a foot on the first step and looked at her. "I'd like it a lot, thanks."

"Come on in. The coffee's already made and it will only take a few minutes to throw something together."

Inside the house, Dusty brought him to the kitchen and poured a cup of coffee, which she placed on the table. "Come and sit down."

"Can I help?"

"No, thanks. I'm just going to microwave some bacon and cut up some fruit."

"Sounds good." Michael sat at the table and picked up his cup. He couldn't stop looking at Dusty. Her movements had a beautiful fluidity, her slender arms, her long legs, the way her head tilted to her tasks. Her hair looked like creamy silk, swaying this way and that, kissing her shoulders, her cheeks.

She was reaching him in a purely female way this morning. Maybe sexual excitement had been lurking in his system all along, but there'd been so many other emotions to deal with since they'd first talked yesterday, he hadn't really acknowledged it.

He was acknowledging it now. Watching Dusty move around the kitchen was an incredible turn-on.

She threw him a glance. "Do you still have family in New York?"

Michael cleared his throat and told his libido to calm down. "My father and brother. Tom's married, so I also have a sister-in-law and two young nieces. How about you?"

"My parents are gone, Michael. Mom first, then Dad three years later."

"I'm sorry."

Dusty sent him a quick smile of thanks, then slipped a plate of bacon into the microwave and set the timer. She turned to the refrigerator and took out melons, strawberries, oranges and bananas.

Michael watched her drop two slices of rye bread into the toaster. Her friendliness this morning was thrilling, much more than he'd hoped for.

"I hope you like your bacon crisp," she remarked when the microwave's bell rang. She brought everything to the table, the fruit, the bacon and the toast.

"Crisp is best," Michael confirmed, eyeing the fruit bowl. "That looks great."

"I like fresh fruit in the morning." Dusty sat down. "Please, help yourself."

He did. Dusty did. They ate, looking at each other across the table every few seconds.

"Your eyes are the color of old gold," Michael said. "Do you know that?"

She smiled. "I've seen them in mirrors for thirty-odd years, Michael."

"You're a very beautiful woman."

Dusty didn't blush easily, but a suspect warmth invaded her cheeks. "Thank you."

"I have a snapshot of you."

Dusty smiled. "There are several of you in my photo album."

His gaze was so intense, Dusty felt an urge to squirm. She reached for her coffee and managed to bring the cup to her lips without spilling any. But it was no more than eight a.m., and Michael was making her think of moonlight and silk sheets.

There was a lot more than the onset of friendship going on between them, Michael knew, positive that Dusty felt it every bit as much as he did. The air around the table felt charged with electricity, a silent crackling that permeated every cell of his body.

"So tell me," he said in a slightly ragged voice, "what have you been doing in Florida, other than reading and walking on the beach? Seen any of the local attractions?"

"I didn't come for the local attractions," Dusty replied quietly. "Winters are long and hard at home. I usually get away from the bad weather for a few weeks in February."

"Are you happy, Dusty?"

She raised a startled eyebrow. "Happy? I . . . suppose so. Are you?"

Michael's eyes stayed leveled on hers. "Not particularly. I've been thinking about finding some other kind of work."

"Leave the law firm?"

"If that idea surprises you, imagine what it would do to my father," Michael said dryly.

"But you're considering it."

"Yes, I'm considering it." Michael grinned suddenly. "Maybe I'll move to Wyoming and become a cowboy."

Dusty laughed. "Yeah, sure."

"I really liked Wyoming that summer."

"It's easy to like in July and August. Put in a winter there and you might change your mind." Dusty stood up. "Would you like some more coffee?" She got the pot and brought it to the table, where she refilled the cup Michael held up, then her own.

"Are you running the Tremayne ranch, Dusty?"

"With some very good help, yes."

"The idea of ranching is almost . . . well, mystical," Michael said as she sat down again.

"A cattle ranch is not at all mystical, believe me," Dusty rebutted. "It's hard work and lots of it."

"But you like it."

"There's nothing else I would rather be doing."

"You're lucky to be in that position."

Dusty's thoughts stalled for a moment. They were speaking of careers. A law career was one to be proud of, but Michael was sounding very disenchanted. "You're really not happy with your profession?"

Michael frowned. "It's hard to explain."

"I didn't mean to pry."

"I didn't see your question as prying. It's just that I'm going through something I really don't understand, and putting it into words is difficult." His eyes were steady on her. "I envy you. I envy anyone who is completely content with their way of life, whatever it is."

"'Completely' might be a bit of an exaggeration," Dusty said softly. "Is anyone ever *completely* content?"

"They should be, don't you think?"

"A lovely concept, but somewhat idealistic, Michael."

He liked the way she said his name. He was slightly punch-drunk, impressed with everything about her, her tawny skin, her leanness, the light in her golden eyes, her voice.

His system was absorbing details, some remembered, some not, the shape of her hands and fingernails, the delicate bone structure of her wrists, the merest hint of a dimple in her left cheek when she spoke and smiled, the lovely arch of her throat.

Underlying her beauty, however, was an extraordinary magnetism, which was definitely nudging Michael's memory. He felt something primal and raw from Dusty, an

earthiness that didn't show in her face. He remembered the
same thing about her from before, but he'd been too young
and inexperienced to act upon it.

With his eyes on her, he ate the last strawberry on his
plate, chewing it slowly, aware that she was watching. He
licked his lips, and Dusty turned her head. His heart stood
still for a moment, then began beating hard enough to hear.
Dusty wasn't looking at him, deliberately, and he was almost positive that he could see the rapid fluttering of the
pulse beat at the base of her throat.

The tension in the kitchen was thick enough to cut, and
getting thicker. Dusty knew it was up to her to do something about it. She stood up. "How about a walk?"

Michael got up, too. "How about a drive?"

"A drive where?"

"Anywhere."

"Oh. Just a drive."

"Would you rather do something else?"

Yes! But we don't dare do it! "No, a drive would
be . . . fine."

"I'll go and borrow my hostess's car."

"I have a rental car in the garage."

Michael nodded. "That'll do, but give me a minute to run
over and tell Cora I'll be gone for a while."

"Yes, of course." While Michael dashed out, Dusty
rubbed the ache in her temples. Every minute in Michael's
presence resulted in another drop in her resistance. If this
kept up, she was apt to knock him to the floor and ravage his
gorgeous body!

Oh, what a disgusting thought. When had she ever been
more jittery around a man? What in hell kind of power did
Michael have? She was getting in way too deep. He had no
irritating or annoying habits, no quirky personality traits.
He was handsome and bright and sincere and sexy, and her
feelings weren't diminishing, they were increasing!

But who, pray tell, was Cora? Was he staying with a
woman?

Dusty went into the bathroom, brushed her teeth, ran a comb through her hair and refreshed her lipstick. Then, with the car keys in her shorts pocket, she returned to the kitchen and quickly cleared the table. The dishes were rinsed and put in the dishwasher before Michael got back.

He came in through the slider. "All set?"

Dusty put on her dark glasses. "All set." She walked to the slider, fully intending to precede Michael through the door.

But he caught her by the arm, his eyes dark and smoky-looking. "I told myself I wouldn't do this. Dusty, do you have any idea what you do to me?"

She couldn't move. She tried but nothing obeyed, not her legs, nor her arms. Maybe she'd been expecting this, maybe not, but she couldn't deny its fascination.

Michael turned slightly, so that he was facing her, standing very close. His hand moved on her arm, slowly, searing skin on its way to her shoulder, then to the back of her neck. Thrills compounded in her system, heated ripples that made normal breathing a physical impossibility.

He took the dark glasses off her face and laid them on the back of a nearby chair, whispering, "It seems like only yesterday..."

Her hand rose to clasp his wrist, the one near her face. "Michael..."

"Don't be afraid. I would never hurt you. Not in any way."

Dusty's system was running wild. "I'm not afraid of you."

"But you are afraid. I can see it in your eyes."

"Not of you."

"Of yourself, then. Of what you're feeling."

"Yes." Her heart was pounding furiously. "I didn't expect this in ... Florida." It was an inane objection, made in a voice as rusty-sounding as an old hinge, but all of her arguments against involvement were losing substance.

He brought his head down, until his mouth was only a breath away from hers. "I don't know what's happening with us, but God, it's exciting. Dusty, if you only knew how I've been feeling. How long it's been . . ."

Dusty knew she should back away. She should deny him, and herself, and do it quickly. Determining this morning that she wasn't capable of living without male companionship was one thing; getting in this deep with Michael was plain foolhardy. She suspected that she could fall very hard this time, and the consequences might not be at all funny.

"Are you feeling what I am?" Michael asked hoarsely.

"I don't want you to kiss me."

He swallowed hard. "Dusty. . ."

"If you kiss me, there'll be no turning back. I don't want that."

"But you care . . . just like I do."

This was much too intense. Drawing a long shaky breath, she took a backward step, breaking all contact with him. "This whole thing is a bad idea, Michael. I shouldn't have asked you in for breakfast. I think I'll skip the drive."

"I've never felt so much for a woman so fast before. Please believe that."

She could say the same about him. But if she fell this time, the crash was going to hurt for an awfully long spell. She wasn't looking for a few dates and a vacation romance, and Michael was. It was as simple as that. She knew that suddenly, as well as she knew her own name. It was a staggering concept. He'd seen her and wanted what he'd missed sixteen years ago.

Michael sensed what was happening, Dusty's complete withdrawal, and he began to talk fast. "I promise to keep my hands to myself. No more passes, Dusty. Just don't tell me to go out that door and leave you alone."

Dusty looked him right in the eye. "How long are you going to be staying with Cora?"

The question took him by surprise, and Michael stared at her. "I'm not sure."

"Another day? A week?"

"A few more days."

Dusty picked up her sunglasses. "Michael, I'm far from being a kid."

"I know you're not."

"You're looking for a quickie affair. I'm not."

"My God..."

"Aren't you?"

He felt himself go pale. "You're making it sound degrading and it's not."

"No, not degrading. I'm not insulted. You're a...very special man. All I'm telling you is that I will not be a part of something that cannot go beyond a few days. Let me be blunt, Michael. I've been down that road before, or one very similar to it. More than once, for that matter." At his wince, Dusty added, "You don't like hearing that, do you? Why is it that men do their ever-lovin' best to bed every attractive woman they meet and then think they should all be virgins?"

"I'm not like that!"

She took in his stricken expression and sighed. "No, maybe not."

"You *are* telling me to go away, aren't you? That's what you're saying. 'Get out of my life, Crowley. You're upsetting my equilibrium.'"

Dusty looked into his wounded blue eyes and suddenly felt deflated. "I don't mean to hurt you." Her own kindly nature was undermining her determination. "Michael, it's best for both of us...not just me. You're thinking about picking up where we left off that summer, and it's just not smart. Not for either of us."

"Give me the courtesy of allowing *me* to decide what's best for *me,* all right?"

His fervor surprised Dusty. There was some anger in his voice, and she wasn't prepared to deal with anger. She, herself, had a very even temper and a knack for speaking her mind without having to be all pumped up from anger or indignation.

"I'm sorry, Michael," she said quietly.

"But you won't see me."

"That's right."

"You're wrong, Dusty. You might have had some bad experiences with a few losers, but..."

"You misunderstand. My bad experiences are my own doing. My decision to elude any more such episodes is also my own doing."

"We meant so much to each other."

"A long time ago, Michael."

Michael had no more arguments. Dusty was unquestionably the most honest woman he'd ever talked to. If there was more time, he knew he could earn her trust. He was not a man she should beware of, but how could he prove that to her in a day or two?

Especially when she was so determined to elude the feelings between them.

He edged to the slider. "I suppose there's no point to further debate. Your mind is made up."

Dusty suddenly felt an almost choking urge to weep, and if there was one thing she wasn't, it was a weeper. The clog in her throat startled her to the point of strained silence.

"Thanks for breakfast."

She made a small throat-clearing sound. "You're welcome."

"See you around."

And then he was gone. One second he was standing within the framework of the slider, the next he wasn't. The air was at once empty and lifeless. *She* was empty and lifeless.

Dusty slowly pulled the slider shut and realized that her hands weren't altogether steady. Her legs, either.

She had already taken one very giant step toward falling for Michael Crowley.

Again.

Four

The day dragged. By midafternoon Dusty couldn't stand it any longer and got into her small rental car and drove to the nearest shopping center. She browsed and window-shopped and finally bought several things she didn't need, just for something to do.

Wondering again if she should cut this holiday short and go home, she walked the length of the indoor mall. Some of the smaller shops were beginning to close, indicating that six o'clock was approaching.

It was obviously time to call it a day, and Dusty left the mall to locate her car in the large and very busy parking lot. Back at the beach house, she put away her purchases, made a smoked turkey sandwich for her supper and sat on the terrace to eat it.

Evenings were fabulous on the Gulf, with the sun going down and silvering the water, with soft, caressing breezes ruffling one's hair, and with the voices of the strollers seeming to be far off and non-echoing. Even the noisy gulls seemed a little less strident at this time of day.

Scanning the scene, Dusty saw the boy and his dog. Smiling because of the duo, she also spotted the elderly gentleman she'd seen with the boy the evening before. On impulse she took off her shoes, rolled up the legs of her slacks and headed for the beach, purposely aiming for the area where the boy and dog were playing.

She said hello to the gray-haired man, who said a bright, chipper "Hello, how are you?" back to her.

"Is that little guy your grandson?"

"Certainly is. Josh is a good lad."

"I've been watching him and his dog playing for several days now. They have a wonderful time, don't they?"

"Yes, indeed. Topper's been in the family as long as Josh has. Josh is my daughter's son and lives in Sarasota. He goes to one of those year-round schools, which is having a break right now."

"I figured something like that."

"Topper gets a real workout when Josh stays with us."

"I can see that. Well, your grandson is an adorable little boy."

"I take it that you like kids."

"Very much."

"Got any of your own?"

Dusty smiled pensively. "Not yet." They were near the water, and Dusty's smile faded when she saw Michael jogging toward her. He was still some distance away but she saw the exact moment when he became aware of her presence. Something gave way in her soul. The sight of him caused an explosion of emotion, and she waited for his approach with an anxious anticipation.

But he ran on past with barely a nod. Dusty's heart turned over, and she called "Michael!" Then she said, "Excuse me" to the boy's grandfather and took off running.

Michael stopped and waited for her to catch up. He saw the distraught expression on her face. "Are you all right?"

Dusty's system was functioning on instinct. Michael had barely acknowledged her, and his coolness felt wrong, artificial. "I'm fine, but . . ."

Resignation replaced his concern. Whatever was happening with the two of them had them both going in circles. He took her hand. "Come on, walk with me."

His hand felt wonderful around hers, big and solid and warm. Dusty suddenly felt very close to him, as though their past relationship had never been interrupted, and the feeling was strange and good and slightly eerie.

"You don't want to like me, do you?" Michael said after a while. They were walking, slowly, just at the edge of the lazy surf.

Dusty sighed. "It would be best."

"You're an unusual woman."

"Because I say what I think?"

"That and . . . other things. Whether you like me or not, Dusty, I like you."

She knew he was telling her the truth. She could actually *feel* his liking.

Or was that warmth in her body a result of her own torn-up feelings?

It was impossible to look at him and not think about how handsome he was, but while she rarely failed to notice a good-looking man, she knew that perfect features were only superficial and not enough.

Michael seemed to have it all, a pleasing personality, incredibly good looks, sex appeal that wouldn't quit, and his feet on the ground, as evidenced by his law career. Stable. A man to respect.

She *was* falling for him and couldn't seem to halt the plunge. Barely able to slow it down, for that matter.

"Tell me about . . . Cora," Dusty said unsteadily.

"Cora? The lady I'm staying with? Sure. What would you like to know?"

"Just who she is."

Michael caught on then and laughed softly. "Cora Potter is one of the greatest women I've ever known. She's kind and generous and uncommonly attractive."

Dusty tried very hard to ignore the jealousy she had no right to feel. "She sounds . . . very nice."

"She is. I've known her all my life."

"Oh, she's an old friend."

"An elderly friend, Dusty. Cora is eighty-one years old."

Dusty turned three shades of red. "I feel rather foolish."

"You weren't comfortable with the idea of my staying with a woman." Michael stopped walking and turned to face Dusty. "You don't want to like me, but you do."

Dusty lifted her chin to look into his eyes. "Yes, I do."

He laid his hand on her cheek. "What are you afraid of?"

"I told you."

"Every relationship is different. Every person is different. Why would you compare me to anyone else you've known?"

"Because *I'm* the same person, Michael, the same with you as . . ."

"No! I won't let you say it. You're not the same with me as you've been with anyone else. People change, Dusty. No one knows that better than I do. No one is the same person today that he was last week, or last year. Our horizons expand with each new acquaintance, each new event."

"I think you're talking about yourself, Michael."

"I'm most definitely talking about myself, but I'm also talking about you. Hasn't meeting me again influenced your life? Meeting you has certainly influenced mine."

"Oh, yes," she sighed. "That's what's so startling, Michael. Meeting again like this."

A smile played with his lips. "Don't look so stricken. Nothing terrible is going to happen just because you and I are attracted to each other."

"But it seems so . . . redundant. Doesn't it strike you that way?"

"Like it all happened before? In a way, yes. But flip the coin to its other side, Dusty. Why *wouldn't* we feel something for each other when we felt so much before? It wasn't you or I who broke us up. We were literally forced apart."

Michael dipped his head, paused to see if she would object, then kissed her lips, a brief mating of mouths that made Dusty's head spin. Objecting hadn't even occurred to her. Rather, she wanted to pull him closer, to prolong the kiss, to hold him and never let him go.

He smiled at her. "Would you like to meet Cora?"

Her reply was low, a little tense. Her new-leaf program wasn't working, not where Michael was concerned. "I'm really not up to meeting anyone right now."

"Whatever you say, but I would like to introduce the two of you."

"Tomorrow?"

"Tomorrow will be great. I'll arrange something, okay?"

"Okay."

Michael looped his arm around her shoulders and started them walking again. Night was falling. The beach was gradually being deserted. Dusty looked back and saw that Josh and his grandfather had gone.

Her system was humming with awareness of the man beside her. She'd been keyed up all day, perhaps hoping for another chance to be with Michael.

"What did you do today?" he questioned.

"Nothing of any consequence. I spent a few hours at a mall this afternoon. What did you do?"

"Wandered, thought, worried. Even forgot to check in with my secretary, but I'm sure she would have called if something important had come up."

Dusty glanced up at him. "What are you worried about, Michael?"

"A lot of things. Myself, where I'm going." He brought his hand up and urged her head down to his shoulder. "You. I kept wondering how to get past your rejection."

Dusty wound her arm around his waist. It felt natural to be walking with Michael, holding each other, talking, reminiscent of that long-ago summer. Her senses were keenly alive, so aware of him, of his height and well-proportioned bulk, of his scent. His thigh caressed hers with every unhurried step, and she was becoming mesmerized with how easily they had found a common rhythm of stride and movement.

They were a match, a pair, she thought. It was as if they had melded in some mysterious way, fitting perfectly into a niche designed for two.

Romantic thoughts. Lovely, romantic feelings. She had it bad for Michael. Or good for Michael. Maybe this was meant to be. Maybe what was happening was out of her hands, not hers to control, or deny.

The avowals and determination she had brought to Florida flitted through her mind, appearing weak and almost fanciful. Reality was walking with a strong, flesh-and-blood man, a man who made her senses sing a siren's song, who brought her spirit to life and urged her soul to dance with gladness.

She tightened her hold on his waist and raised her face to his, her eyes glowing with emotion. Michael's heartbeat sped up and he pressed his lips to hers, taking their lush fullness, tasting their honeyed flavor. Her tongue met his halfway, and her free hand slid up his chest to the back of his head, where her fingers wove into his hair.

She turned, bringing their bodies together, her aching breasts to his chest, her hips to his. His arms brought her closer, wedging them tightly together. Their first kiss demanded another, and neither could breathe without gasps.

"Oh, Dusty, oh, honey," he whispered raggedly, and ran his hands down her back to her hips, bringing her even closer, molding her to the fiery heat of his arousal. "Kissing you, holding you...I can't tell you what it means to me."

"Come to the house," she whispered while dropping kisses on his chin, his throat, his mouth. Her hands were in his hair, greedy in their possession, hungry in their exploration. "Give me a few minutes, then come."

"Anything you say. Five minutes?"

The tip of her tongue circled his lips. "Fifteen."

He kissed her almost savagely, his own desire magnified by hers. "Fifteen minutes," he murmured by way of agreement. He would have done anything she might ask at that moment—swim the Gulf, climb tall mountains, anything.

They moved apart, reluctantly, their hands sliding down the other's arm and then clinging until the last possible second. "I'll be waiting," she said softly.

"I'll be there."

Dusty sped away, and looked back to see Michael heading for the fourth house down from hers. Her house was dark, but Cora's had several lighted windows. Slogging through the sand, she mounted her steps out of breath. Her heart was beating so hard it seemed to be tripping over itself. She opened the slider, stepped in, closed the door at her back and then stood there, suddenly stunned to complete immobility.

Was she actually going to do this? *She had invited Michael to her house to make love!* He knew it, she knew it. In his arms, it had seemed like the only way. Now...

"Oh, damn," she moaned, and flipped on the wall switch for a light and shoved herself away from the glass door. She needed a shower, in any case, and began shedding her clothes on the way to the bathroom.

Her blood was flowing hot and fast, with every nerve ending sensually sensitized. She was in love, more in love than she'd ever been. She wanted Michael with an overwhelming passion, but sexual desire wasn't the only ingredient in her torment of feelings. This was the real thing, and she was asking for the worst kind of heartache a woman could suffer. Their time together could be measured in days. How many? One more, two? If she denied anything further between them, she would still return to Wyoming unhappy; making love with him would only intensify her misery.

This was what they should have had sixteen years ago, only they'd been too young. They weren't too young now. They were... just right. Perfect for one another.

She couldn't do it, she *wouldn't* do it. When Michael arrived... Oh, damn, how could she reverse herself now? Was she insane? Michael would think she was, and could she blame him? She had invited him, not the other way around!

Dusty dried off with trembling hands. She dressed, choosing a loose, unstructured dress that nearly reached her ankles. It had a high circular neckline and was barely feminine, let alone seductive. It was the kind of thing she liked to lounge around in, nothing she would normally wear for a meeting with a man.

It had been in her mind to dress alluringly. A shower, perfumed body lotion and something scant and sexy.

With a nervous eye on the clock, she hurriedly brushed her hair and applied some makeup.

In exactly fifteen minutes Michael rapped at the glass slider. Dusty took a deep breath, composed her expression and walked through the house.

He, too, had showered, she saw. His dark hair glistened with moisture. He'd shaved, and his jaw was clean and shiny. He was wearing a pair of white slacks and a white shirt, partially unbuttoned, which he hadn't bothered to tuck into his pants.

He was carrying a small bottle of wine.

When he saw her, he smiled and slid the door open. "I borrowed some wine from Cora's cellar." Stepping in, he caught the back of Dusty's head in his hand and kissed her, slowly but thoroughly.

Something wept within her. She laid a hand on his chest and closed her eyes. The strength to refuse him, and herself, was so puny it was pathetic. How could she muster disseminated pockets of common sense, when everything else she was wanted tonight with Michael?

"I'll get some glasses," she said huskily. "Do you need a corkscrew?"

"I already opened it." Michael plucked the loosened cork from the bottle. He followed Dusty to the kitchen, where she got two tulip glasses from a cabinet.

Michael poured the wine and held out a glass to her. He raised his. "To us, Dusty. To you and me."

There was excitement in his eyes. Her feelings went way back, bridging time. He was the hero of her youth, the knight in shining armor who'd been ripped from her arms without fulfillment. Their separation had been sensible but cruel. She bore no ill will for her parents; they'd been good people and had sincerely believed in their actions. Pragmatically Dusty agreed: Seventeen was too young for marriage. She and Michael had had nothing of their own, nothing with which to begin a life together.

Nothing except love. Her heart swelled. "To us, Michael," she whispered, and touched her glass to his. They each took a sip.

Michael took the glass from her and set both of them on the counter. He slid his hands around her waist and brought her forward. "I've been dreaming of this."

They searched each other's eyes. "I think I have, too."

"You're so beautiful, you take my breath." He lowered his head to brush a slow-burning kiss across her forehead. His lips traveled down one cheek, then lingered at first one corner of her mouth, then the other.

Her heart felt like a speeding train. Her breasts were heavy and aching. She dampened her lips and placed her hands on his chest. She had never wanted a man more, never. Her past romances had been insignificant, no comparison at all. This was not a mistake, it couldn't be. She sensed Michael's feelings as genuine, and felt weak and pliant from her own.

His mouth settled on hers, angling for the perfect fit. Dusty snuggled closer and wrapped her arms around his waist. His tongue touched hers gently, and she felt his restraint, as though he was trying not to rush her. That small gift was pleasing, indicating a great deal about the man giving it.

She stopped thinking then. The kiss was heady, dizzying her mind. Michael's hands moved over her, slowly, unhurriedly. Her hands stroked up his back and then down again. Their kisses became briefer in duration, hungrier.

The warmth of her skin came through her clothing. She was so female, voluptuously generous. Michael sought the splendor of her mouth, again and again, feeling that he could kiss her forever.

Dusty brought her hands from around him, squeezed them in between their bodies and slid them up his chest. At his collar she caressed his throat, the back of his neck. Her

fingertips glided over his jaw and ears and into his hair.
"Oh, Michael," she whispered.

"How I want you."

"I know."

Their voices were low and husky, constructed purely of
emotion. They were so alone, far, far away from responsi-
bilities and the mundane chores of ordinary life. That they
had been drawn from distant corners of the country to this
little rental house on a Florida beach seemed magical. That
they were together again after so long was bewitching, en-
trancing.

Dusty undid the few closed buttons on Michael's shirt and
nuzzled her face against his chest, inhaling deeply the warm,
clean smell of his skin. His hands, she realized dimly, were
seeking an entrance to her dress.

The dress had been a bad choice; it had no openings.

She took his hand. "Let's get out of the kitchen."

He nodded, and together they made their way to Dusty's
bedroom. She snapped off lights as they went, leaving the
house dark behind them. A soft glow came from the small
decorative lamp on the dresser. Letting go of Michael's
hand, Dusty yanked the drapes closed over the tinted windowpanes.

Then, dampening her lips, she turned to Michael's gaze
and slowly drew the inconvenient dress over her head. He
swallowed. Her bra was soft and lacy, shaped into round-
ness by her breasts, her panties a mere scrap. Her body was
beautiful, lighter-skinned than her legs and arms.

In the diffused, feeble light emitted by the pretty little
lamp, Michael shed his shirt, letting it slide from his shoulders and arms to be caught by one hand and placed carelessly on the room's one chair.

They moved closer together, Dusty taking two steps, Michael three. He put his hands on her waist and closed his
eyes. The sensation of her bare skin was intoxicating. His
hands glided upward, while hers moved over his chest.

She made a small sound when he touched her breasts, one
with each hand, and he opened his eyes to see into hers. Her

pleasure at his touch was like a sudden shot of adrenaline, and he quickly unhooked the front clasp of her bra. Her breasts spilled out of the lace, full and lush, as pale as ivory except for their rich, rosy crests.

He was suddenly dry-mouthed and dizzy with desire, wondering if he would last long enough to give her satisfaction. Neglecting his sex life for two years hadn't been important to him, but cheating Dusty was unthinkable.

He brought her close and kissed her mouth, uniting their bodies, groaning at the delicious shock of her breasts against his chest. She moved in his arms, rubbing against him, her tongue seeking his. Her hands located the button on the waist of his pants, then the zipper in his fly. Undone, the pants slipped down. Dusty was stunned, then pleased to realize that he'd ignored underwear. Laughing softly deep in her throat, she caressed his maleness.

Michael was practically seeing stars. Staying cool was a massive effort. Breathing hard, he urged her toward the bed. While she turned it down, he freed his feet of his pants and got a condom out of a pocket.

But he laid it on the bed stand, because he had something other than his own fulfillment in mind.

Dusty turned from the bed, her eyes smoky with passion, and slid down her panties. Michael's total nudity was a sight to behold, and she took her time in a long look. "You're incredible," she said huskily. "I used to wonder."

"I lay awake many a night thinking about you."

"We were so young, but I had younger friends who experimented. Why didn't we?"

Michael slowly shook his head. "Honor? Standards? Dusty, I don't know. Are you sorry we didn't?"

"I was after you left. I cried buckets."

"Did anyone care?" Michael closed the gap between them and tenderly caressed the curve of her cheek with his forefinger, thinking of his father's sternness during that stressful period.

"I don't know. Mom and Dad seemed very subdued for a long time, so maybe they cared. Looking back, I'm sure they did. At the time I was so full of resentment, I wasn't concerned with anyone's feelings but my own, but I'm sure they got no joy out of breaking us up."

"I guess they weren't wrong. What could I have given you? I had no skills, no way to make a decent living."

Dusty sighed. "No, they weren't wrong. And it's probably best that we didn't go too far. I might have gotten pregnant."

Michael's expression became poignant. "Yes, you might have." In the next instant he moaned and gathered her into a fierce embrace. Tears stung his eyes, and he buried his face in her hair.

Their desire for each other seemed to explode then. They fell to the bed, arms and legs intertwined, kisses falling aimlessly. Dusty's brain seemed ready to burst with an urge to put her feelings into words, to tell him how deeply she was affected. She was thinking about love, feeling love, and she wanted to share everything with him.

Something stopped her. Even dazed with passion she knew it was too soon. There were steps to a relationship, and they had already jumped quite a few of them. As hot as it was between them, if Michael had been a complete stranger they would not be in bed together within days of their meeting. Eventually, yes. Dusty was too aware of her own physicality to deny the power of Michael's overwhelming chemistry.

She wouldn't let herself think beyond tonight, although, in the back of her mind, she truly believed that Michael was as moved by genuine, durable emotions as she was. There was too much evidence to think otherwise. His touch was exquisite, the hand slipping down her body both gentle and commanding. His caring was almost tangible; she was not merely a willing woman to him.

His mouth left hers to trail downward, nestling without haste into the curve of her throat, then dropping again. Breathing through parted lips, Dusty closed her eyes as his tongue wet a nipple. She felt his mouth open around it and then a gentle sucking, a tugging sensation that she felt clear down to her toes. A throaty "Oh, Michael" wasn't nearly adequate praise for what he was making her feel, but it was all she could manage.

He kissed her stomach, her thighs, repeatedly, and then parted her legs for a more intimate kiss. Dusty's heart leaped into her throat. His tongue was hot and wet and doing delicious things to her. The heat rose in her body; the pleasure increased until she was moaning and unable to lie still.

It happened quickly then, the intensity of a completion that fogged her brain and brought tears to her eyes. Wave after wave of pleasure, until she was weak and limp and emotionally drained.

Michael moved up in the bed and wrapped his arms around her, bringing her head to his chest. He felt her tears and the trembling that gradually dissipated. He kissed the top of her head and stroked her back. She lay in his arms, unmoving, for a very long time.

Dusty raised up to an elbow and looked at him. His generous lovemaking was extremely gratifying, and she intended to return the favor. Saying nothing, but continuing to look into his eyes, she slowly wound a lock of his hair around her forefinger. Dipping her head, she began dropping small kisses on his face. She rubbed her nose against his. She caught his bottom lip between her teeth and nipped gently. Her hand slid down his cheek, his jaw, his throat and chest, down farther to the tight muscles of his abdomen. He was fully aroused, he had been all along, and she took his manhood in her hand, which was as pleasurable for her as it was for him.

Michael groaned. "Do you have a condom?" she whispered.

"On the nightstand."

Dusty glanced over her shoulder, saw the item and then reached for it. Smiling at Michael, interpreting his strange expression as surprise, she rolled the soft rubber into place. For a second she wanted to mention inhibitions, to tell Michael that she had very few, but it didn't seem like the most auspicious occasion to remind a man that he wasn't the first.

As far as inhibitions went, if Michael ever wanted to know, Dusty had no qualms about listing every single man she'd ever been interested in. She would not pretend or lie about the matter, not to anyone. She was not ashamed of her romantic entanglements, just disappointed and a little regretful, for her own sake.

But she had the feeling all of that was behind her. Michael was everything she'd ever wanted in a man. She'd been wise enough at seventeen to recognize his value, and maybe losing him then was what had set her on the path of looking for a replacement.

Some people couldn't be replaced. Some feelings were impossible to duplicate; what she had felt for Michael at seventeen had been unique. She knew that now.

"You're a temptress," Michael accused thickly, as her hands moved over him.

"Am I?"

"I can take no more."

"No?" She bent and placed a lingering kiss to a very sensitive spot.

Rising up with a powerful push, Michael tipped her onto her back. He laid on top of her, pinning her seductive hands to the bed. Her legs parted willingly.

"If you can take no more, what are you planning to do about it?" she whispered.

"What do you think?"

It was an exciting game. Dusty licked her lips. "I'll fight you."

"How?"

"Just try to thread a moving needle, just try it!"

Michael threw back his head and roared with laughter. She was spread-eagled, her hands held down by his, her legs spread wide, and her impossible challenge was no more than a spurt of sensual teasing. He loved it.

His expression sobered. Looking deeply into her eyes, he adjusted his position enough for penetration. Her pleasurable reaction was all over her face. He slid into her heat very slowly, dragging out the moment and tension to its fullest.

"What was that comment about a moving needle?" he whispered.

She opened her mouth and took a big gulp of air. "I don't remember." Her face was getting flushed, her skin sweaty. "Do it, Michael. Make love to me. I need you."

"Oh, baby," he groaned and let go of her hands to burrow them beneath her hips.

It was over in minutes, with both of them drenched in perspiration and gasping for breath. They lay locked together then, lost in a marvelous world of supreme satisfaction. Gradually Dusty's heartbeat returned to normal; eventually Michael gained the strength to move.

Reality came in small doses at first, then in a rushing tide.

Wondering if he dared to start talking about something permanent for them, Michael raised his head and regarded her rather solemnly. Dusty returned the scrutiny, also somberly. It had been earthshaking between them, and both knew it.

"What does a man say about such perfection?" Michael murmured.

"What does a woman say?" They had climaxed at exactly the same moment, a rarity among lovers.

"Dusty... this is important."

"Yes."

"*We're* important."

"Yes!" Her heart soared. She needed no further affirmation at the moment, and she pulled Michael's head down for a kiss.

Later, when they were merely lying in bed, with Dusty's backside nestled against Michael and his arms around her, she thought about the future. There would be problems, of course, he lived so far from Wyoming.

She yawned. Every problem had a solution, if one wanted it bad enough. She and Michael, together, would work it out.

Michael glanced at the bedside clock. "It's very late." He was curled around Dusty's warm and relaxed body, her hips in his lap, and she moved languidly, making a small, breathy sound that resembled "Hmm."

"I should be going," Michael whispered.

"All right," Dusty said on a long, contented sigh. "Come for breakfast in the morning."

"I'll be here." He kissed her shoulder, then brought her chin around to kiss her lips. "I'll never forget tonight, Dusty."

She smiled dreamily. "Nor will I."

He kissed her again. "Sleep well." He got out of bed, found his clothes and dressed. A final look at Dusty brought a contented smile to his face. She was sound asleep, beautiful in the moonlight.

He let himself out and trudged through the sand to Cora's house.

Five
———

Dusty opened her eyes, saw that the room was just beginning to lighten, and forced her eyelids closed again. Her body was marvelously loose and mellow, without a drop of tension anywhere to be found. She smiled and took a long, languorous breath.

Michael . . . wonderful, beautiful Michael. She loved him madly, with every fiber of her being. She had never really been in love before, how could she have thought she was? This was the genuine article, the emotion that inspired poets, and she had never even come close to it with another man.

"Michael," she whispered, adoring even his name. She stretched, lazily, and knew that she wasn't going to go back to sleep. Throwing aside the sheet, she got up and stretched again. A shower? Coffee?

It was very early, much too early to begin the day. She laughed softly.

Donning a robe as she went and padding barefoot through the house, Dusty approached the slider and looked out. No one was on the beach.

Going to the kitchen, she put on a pot of coffee. There was a low-key hum of happiness in her system, a lovely sensation. She felt too good to do nothing, too alive, and she decided on some fresh air now and a shower later.

Leaving the coffee to brew by itself, Dusty returned to the bedroom and exchanged her robe for shorts and T-shirt and canvas shoes. She brushed her teeth, but merely finger-combed her hair, ignoring the hairbrush and array of cosmetics on the sink counter.

A long walk in the cool morning air was on her mind when she went through the slider to the terrace. She stopped to breathe it in, and her gaze fell on the novel she'd been trying to wade through, lying on the table where she had left it.

It was a very dull story with not particularly good writing, and she probably wouldn't finish it. A smile lifted her lips. Why would she waste time reading about romance when she was living it for herself?

Dusty picked up the book. Her bookmark was inserted about a third of the way through the nearly four hundred pages. No, she probably wouldn't finish it, but she would take it back to Wyoming with her and give it to Louise Myers. Mrs. Myers was an elderly semibedridden friend who read a great deal. Dusty often loaded up a box with paperbacks and brought it over to the Myers's place for Louise.

Laying the book down again, Dusty skipped from the terrace, jogged down to the beach and headed north.

"Michael?" The door of his room opened a crack. "Michael, the phone's for you."

He'd thought he'd heard a telephone ringing but wasn't sure if it was for real or part of a dream. He sat up and glanced at the clock, registering an unholy four-forty a.m. on the digital dial. "Thanks, Mary."

There was a phone on the stand by his bed, and he picked it up, wondering who on earth would be calling him at this hour. "This is Michael Crowley."

"Michael? Tom. Listen, Dad's had a heart attack."

Michael's grogginess vanished as a surge of adrenaline hit his system. "When?"

"A few hours ago. He's in the hospital."

"Is it bad?"

"Very. I think you'd better get back here."

For a few painful seconds Michael's brain went into stall. Plane schedules and reservations, what was happening in New York, and Dusty, all whirled around without a whole lot of sense.

He recovered. "I'll catch the first flight out."

"Come directly to the hospital. Sacred Heart. The cardiovascular wing. That's where I'm calling from."

"I'll be there."

Michael put the phone down, and it was then that the enormity of the situation really hit him. His father. A heart attack. A *serious* heart attack.

He rubbed the back of his neck, trying to think. A knock at the bedroom door brought his head around. Cora came in, wearing a robe and an anxious expression. "What is it, Michael?"

"Dad's in the hospital. Heart attack."

"Oh, dear."

Michael fumbled in the drawer of the bed stand for the phone book. "I've got to catch the first flight out."

"Yes, of course. Michael, make reservations for Mary and me, also. Your father was there for me when George became ill, and I want to be there for him."

"That's very kind, Cora, but..."

"No, please, I insist. I couldn't possibly stay here and worry."

It didn't matter to Michael who went along. He was swamped with fear for his father, and if Cora would feel better about the whole thing in New York than in Florida, that was fine with him. As for Mary, she traveled on Cora's schedule.

He finally got through to the airline and reserved three seats for a flight they would just barely have time to make, then dressed with the speed of light. He knew Cora and Mary were doing the same. There was no time to spare.

Throwing things into his suitcase, he remembered Dusty again. He couldn't go off without seeing her! It would take about five minutes to run over to her house, and it was five minutes he had to use, even if he left Cora's house without his luggage.

Michael ran into the hall and yelled, "I'll be right back, Cora!"

She came out of her room puzzled over Michael racing down the stairs like a wild man. Mary poked her head out of her own room. "What's happening?"

"I think Michael's going over to tell his lady friend that he has to leave."

"I think he really likes her, Cora."

"Yes, he does. I wish she and I had met. I have a feeling she is very important to our Michael. Now, hurry. We must be ready when he returns."

Michael ran as hard as he could, reaching Dusty's house in seconds. He tried the terrace slider and found it still unlocked, so he pushed it open and rushed through the house, fully expecting to see Dusty in bed.

The room was empty. He took a quick peek into the bathroom. "Dusty?" He raced through the house to the kitchen and saw the fresh pot of coffee. She couldn't be far, probably on the beach.

He went out to the terrace and frantically scanned the area. Far off, way to the north, the miniature figure of someone walking alone was barely discernible. He couldn't tell if it was Dusty or not.

It didn't matter. Even if he knew for a fact that the person was Dusty, he didn't have the time to catch up with her.

Michael looked around for something to write on. There was nothing on the terrace, except for Dusty's book. He tore through the house again, hoping to spot a piece of paper and a pencil.

He had to let her know. He couldn't just go off without an explanation. The phone! Hurrying to the phone, Michael examined it for a number and his heart nearly stopped. It was one of those portable models and nothing was written on it. He cursed and began yanking drawers open. Without a phone number, a written message was his only hope.

Finally, he spotted a ballpoint pen on a small table. No paper, though. Nothing! Not even a damned newspaper so he could rip off a corner or something.

Dusty's book!

Hurrying back outside, Michael opened the book and saw the bookmark. Relieved, he scribbled a message, writing very small because of the tiny available space: *Dusty, my father's had a heart attack. Am flying home at once. My telephone number is 555-9878. Call me! All my love, Michael.*

He closed the book with the marker protruding an inch above the text, feeling that he had found the perfect place to leave a note. Anyone in the middle of a book couldn't possibly miss a message written on its page marker.

Then he took the terrace steps at a dead run. He *had* to make that plane!

The sun was up and warming the sand when Dusty got back to the house. She felt fantastic, energized from exercise, thrilled to think of the day ahead. Beyond that, nothing was certain, but she knew in her heart that she and Michael had a future together. It wouldn't be easy, not with so many states between their respective homes, but she was confident they would work it out.

She went directly to the bathroom and turned on the shower. And then she did something she never did, she sang! While she shampooed and soaped, she belted out a few country classics, laughing at her efforts because singing was definitely not her forte.

But it was fun, and she felt so damned good. So alive!

Drying off, Dusty searched through the closet for the perfect outfit. She wanted to knock Michael's socks off this morning.

And then his pants!

She giggled.

Life was crazy and wonderful and she felt light-headed enough to fly.

She fixed her hair and took great pains with her makeup, finally putting on a sweet but sexy sundress in an array of brilliant colors. It looked great. *She* looked great, she decided happily in front of the mirror.

But the bedroom didn't look so hot, she saw, and she set to work, getting out clean sheets, making the bed, picking up after herself.

Finally everything was ready for Michael's arrival. Humming under her breath, Dusty went to the kitchen and poured herself a cup of coffee. Along with fresh fruit this morning, she decided, she would prepare her special scrambled eggs, which were mixed with bits of smoked sausage, mushrooms and green onions.

Dusty got out the ingredients and then sliced the sausage, which had to be slightly browned before the onions were sautéed. The mushrooms would be added to the pan with the beaten eggs, and then everything would be stirred and cooked to perfection. Michael would like it.

When everything was sliced and diced, ready for the pan, Dusty took her coffee to the table and sat down. After a few minutes, she got up and flipped the TV on to catch the news. No newspaper was an annoyance, but getting a paper involved a drive to the market, and she didn't want to leave the house right now.

The coffee in her cup was beginning to get cold when she checked the time. Michael was an early riser, just as she was. What was keeping him?

Dusty turned off the TV and went out to the terrace. The beach was becoming active, a normal morning. Michael wasn't in sight, though, so he hadn't decided to take a jog before coming to breakfast.

She went back inside, dumped the cold coffee down the drain and refilled her cup. She drank part of it at the table, but when it, too, began cooling, she got up with a frown. Something was wrong. Michael should have been here by now.

Dusty went back outside. The morning was glorious, but a tiny seed of discomfort had sprouted in her midsection. Kicking off her sandals, she left the terrace and walked in the direction of Cora Potter's home.

It was a beautiful place, large and sprawling and glistening white in the sunlight. Its landscaping was magnificent, scrupulously cared for.

But it was completely silent. Was the household sleeping late?

That must be it. Michael was merely sleeping in. He had gotten little sleep last night, after all.

But she hadn't slept very much, either, and she had awakened even earlier than usual.

Dusty went back to her own house and sat on the terrace. Michael would be coming any minute now, she told herself. She would not rush to any foolish conclusions just because he hadn't arrived when she had expected.

An hour went by, each minute dragging. Dusty sat there, staring at the beach, at the people passing by, seeing everything, registering very little. Even the appearance of Josh and Topper couldn't warm the chill developing in her system.

Something was very wrong. Michael wasn't coming.

No! Dusty jumped up. This wasn't happening! *She* was the one who was wrong! Her overactive imagination was devising the worst possible scenario. Michael was merely late! He had a good reason, which he would tell her all about when he got here!

In fact, she was so positive that he would show up at any minute, she would go ahead with breakfast.

She took her time, browning the sausage very slowly, then adding the chopped green onions. It smelled delicious, and she took a minute to check out the slider window before pouring the egg mixture into the pan.

When it was done, Dusty bit down on her bottom lip until it hurt. Michael was not coming, and she could cook any damned thing she wanted, or lie to herself until she was blue in the face. *He was not coming!*

Nausea rolled in her stomach. She had done it again, fallen too fast, given everything to the wrong man.

She had to calm herself. Any number of things might have happened. Judging Michael too quickly was unfair to him and only causing herself pain.

Dusty turned off the stove and pushed the pan to a cold burner. Leaving the house, she trudged back down the beach to the Potter house. Only this time, she mounted its elegant staircase to its elegant terrace, and with a determined expression, she knocked on its elegant glass doors. After a second, she spotted the button of a doorbell, and she pushed on it, hearing an immediate chiming from inside the house.

No other sound reached her ears. No one came to the door.

She laid on the button, and the inside chimes rang and rang, as melodic as the bells of a church on a clear Sunday morning.

There was no one here, not Michael, not Cora Potter.

A strange numbness befell Dusty. She stood there, trying to digest, trying to understand. Michael was gone. Even the lady of the house, Cora Potter, was gone. Why? Where? An errand? Why wouldn't Michael have come by and told her that he had to cancel their breakfast plans?

What should she do now?

Had there been some sort of emergency? Maybe Cora had fallen ill and Michael had driven her to the doctor.

Darn, he couldn't even call her, Dusty realized suddenly. The telephone in her house was listed in the rental agency's company name. Its number and usage had been given to her only after she had paid a sizeable deposit. There'd been no reason to give the number to Michael, and unless he knew the rental agent's name, which was unlikely, he wouldn't be able to get it from information.

Of course, Cora Potter might know the rental agent's name.

This was really very weird. Dusty cupped her hands around her face and tried to see in through the glass doors of Cora's home.

"Can I help you, Miss?"

Dusty jumped back, as guilty as if she'd been attempting to break and enter. A heavyset man holding a pair of pruning shears was standing near the terrace, eyeing her curiously.

"I was looking for... Cora Potter."

"She's gone away, Miss."

"Gone?"

The man came closer to the steps. "I'm the gardener. There was a note on the toolshed door this morning. Her and Mary took a trip."

"Mary?"

"The woman who lives with her."

"Did she say anything about her houseguest, a Mr. Crowley?"

"No, but there's no one here now."

The man looked rather disinterested. He'd passed on the only message he had, apparently, and had nothing more to say. Dispiritedly Dusty crossed the terrace to the steps and started down. "Thanks for the information."

"You're welcome."

Dusty walked with her head down. There was no emergency, there wasn't even a simple errand. Cora, and whoever Mary was, had gone off on a trip, which left Michael to go off somewhere, too. The gardener had said it plain enough: "There's no one here."

Michael was gone. Without a goodbye, without one single word. He must have known he was leaving last night. He *had* to have known. In all of her relationships, friendships, battles or what have you with men, none had done something like this to her.

But then, she had known them all much better than she knew Michael.

Michael was a first. Despite their joke of a marriage, Michael was a pickup, as close to a one-night stand as she had ever gotten.

He was so clever with his sincere expressions and remarks. My God, how could she have been so taken in?

You deserve everything you're getting! You're a fool, you've always been a fool, and instead of improving your interaction with men, you're slipping to an even lower rung!

Tears filled Dusty's eyes, and she angrily brushed them away. Mr. Right, hah! Mr. Jerk of the Month was more like it.

She couldn't even vow not to be so stupid again. Her soul was full of it, though, and she knew without putting it into words that no man would get so close again. Where there had been life in her body, now there was ice.

I'll never forget tonight, Dusty.

Nor will I.

She'd never spoken truer words. Nothing would make her forget last night and Michael Crowley, nothing! Revenge was impossible. He was probably back in his cushy New York office, conducting business as though he hadn't destroyed a woman in Florida.

The bastard. The rotten, lousy, lying *bastard!*

Dusty marched into her house, took one look at the mess in the kitchen and cursed again, using words she normally despised and avoided. She began cleaning up, dumping the pan of eggs into the garbage disposal, putting things away.

Then she stopped. She couldn't stay here. Not one minute longer than it took her to pack.

There were clauses in her rental agreement. If the house was not left in the same condition as it had been upon her arrival, the agency would keep her very healthy deposit.

"To hell with it," Dusty muttered, and went to the telephone. She was in no mood to clean a house. She looked up the airline's number and dialed it. "What's your next flight out that will get me to Casper, Wyoming? I already have a ticket."

An hour later Dusty was ready to leave. Her suitcases were packed, she was dressed for traveling. She would be home by tonight.

Had she forgotten anything?

Making a quick tour of the house, she spotted her book on the terrace table. With a cynical expression, she went out to get it. She didn't want the damned thing, but Louise Myers might enjoy it.

Unzipping one of her suitcases, Dusty wedged the book inside and zipped it shut again.

Next year, if she was in the traveling mood, she would go to Arizona!

Nancy and Luke were surprised by Dusty's early return. She mumbled something about being bored with Florida and let it go at that. The Wilkenses had been planning to take a little trip themselves, only delaying their departure until Dusty was back. She told them to go ahead with their plans, preferring to be alone in the house for a while, although she knew that brooding would do little good.

She was just so filled with anger, and she didn't need any witnesses to the periodic bouts of hot tears that struck without warning.

She'd been home for five days and the Wilkenses had been gone for four when the telephone rang at nine in the evening. It hadn't occurred to her that Michael might call; his departure from Florida had been too final to think he might suddenly develop a conscience and attempt to talk to her.

Listlessly she picked up the phone. "Tremayne Ranch."

"Dusty?"

Shock froze her, but only for a second. She spoke calmly but coldly. "I have nothing to say to you. Please do not call again."

The sound of Dusty hanging up in his ear startled Michael. He held the phone out and stared at it incredulously.

Then, clicking the mechanism to get another dial tone, he punched out Dusty's Wyoming number again. He'd been worried because she hadn't called him, as he'd asked her to do in his note, but reaching her by telephone in Florida was impossible. He didn't have the number of that portable phone in her rental house, and he'd finally admitted, after exhausting every avenue, that there was no way to get it.

With everything going on in New York, he probably hadn't been thinking very straight. It had just occurred to him, not five minutes ago, that someone at the Tremayne Ranch was bound to have Dusty's Florida number.

He hadn't expected her to answer, though, and he sure as hell hadn't expected her to hang up on him, once she had!

She didn't answer again. He sat through a dozen rings, questioning her attitude, becoming angry, then sick at heart. What was wrong? She'd been so warm and loving, and now she didn't even want to talk to him? It didn't make sense.

Michael put the phone down and stared broodingly at the instrument. Was she back to considering him a mistake? She had some kind of hang-up about mistakes with men, that much was clear. But why would she be so rude about it? My God, he hadn't *wanted* to leave Florida so abruptly. Surely she wasn't upset about that.

No, of course she wasn't. It was something else. She'd had second thoughts about their speeding relationship, or some damned thing.

Michael's expression became grim. This was not the end of it for him and Dusty, far from it. It was time he got his act together, time for him to do something about the dissatisfaction and discontent he'd been living with. It would take a little time, he had a lot of loose ends in New York.

But Dusty was going to explain right to his face about tonight, about why she'd told him not to call again, and why she'd hung up on him.

Yeah, that was best. They would talk face-to-face.

Six

Four weeks later...

Dusty was walking from the barn to the house when she spotted the mud-spattered black Bronco parked in the driveway. It was a chilly, partially overcast day, and Dusty was wearing a sheepskin vest over a long-sleeved shirt, faded jeans, boots and her favorite old hat.

She glanced at the Bronco as she crossed the backyard lawn, not particularly interested in it. It had a Wyoming plate, but she didn't recognize the vehicle and thought that one of Nancy's friends might have dropped in.

But Nancy met her at the back door. "There's someone here to see you."

"Who?" Dusty went in, took off her hat and hung it on one of the hooks in the entry hall. That's when she noticed that Nancy's seams were close to bursting. Nancy Wilkens was forty-three, a pretty woman with light brown hair and eyes.

She was also Dusty's best friend, although Dusty hadn't said a word about Michael for quite some time after her return from Florida. Eluding Nancy's naturally curious nature couldn't last for long, however, and in a weak moment one evening, Dusty spilled enough of her fiasco in Florida that Nancy understood why she'd been so down in the dumps.

"Michael Crowley," Nancy whispered, her eyes as big as saucers.

Dusty felt as though something huge and heavy had just slammed into her stomach. Her face lost color, and for a moment she wondered if she was going to do something totally ridiculous, like sinking to her knees.

"I don't believe it," she scoffed faintly. Michael, here? Impossible!

"Believe it, Dusty. He's sitting in the living room. Incidentally, he's gorgeous!"

"Fat lot of good that does anyone." She was getting her wind back, and a little spirit. "I'm not sure I'm going to see him. He's got some nerve! I told him on the phone to leave me alone."

"Well, you can't just *not* see him," Nancy whispered. Dusty raised an eyebrow. "Can you?"

"Oh, I could do it, all right." Dusty's eyes narrowed. "But now that he's here, maybe I should just march in there and tell him what a jerk he is."

"Oh, Dusty," Nancy said forlornly. "He's come an awfully long way."

"He gets around, apparently," Dusty drawled dryly. "He means nothing to me, Nancy, not this much." She held up her thumb and forefinger, less than an inch apart. "And he has no right to barge in like this."

Nancy sighed. "Probably not. Well, I can't tell you how to treat the man, but he is waiting."

Dusty was thinking of her appearance. No makeup, hat-flattened hair, worn-out jeans, scuffed boots. She was over the crying spells. Her heart had toughened considerably in the past month, and whatever Michael or any other man might think of her was totally immaterial.

"I'll go and see what he wants," she said in a hard tone of voice.

"Maybe you should invite him to dinner. One more plate on the table wouldn't matter."

Dusty gave her friend a truly scathing glare. Nancy cooked for everyone on the place, eight people, and her first impulse with a visitor was always to invite him or her to dinner.

"Just a thought," Nancy said quickly. "Forget I mentioned it." Dusty started from the kitchen. "Uh . . . if you'd like, I could keep him busy for a few minutes while you . . . uh . . . tidy up."

Dusty whirled. "I have no intention of 'tidying up' for that man! He can take me the way I am or not at all. Frankly, I prefer the *not at all!*"

Nancy drew herself up. "Well, exxccuuse me!"

Both women stared, then started giggling. Nancy put her hand over her mouth to stem the tide, and Dusty ran for the entry and buried her face in a jacket on one of the hooks.

"Nancy, stop it," she finally hissed, wiping her eyes on the sleeve of her shirt.

"*You* stop it. What are we giggling about, anyway?"

Dusty leaned against the wall and put her head back. "God, I have no idea. This is not funny."

"No?"

They were off again, laughing almost hysterically. Dusty finally calmed down enough to whisper, "What am I going to do? I *should* go in there and bat him alongside the head."

Nancy nearly fell on the floor in another paroxysmy of silent laughter. She dried her eyes. "Look, you can't walk into that room and start giggling."

"I'd die!"

"You need to go in there with dignity."

"Yes, dignity. I need to show that jerk that what he did in Florida doesn't mean diddly. Actually I should act like I didn't even notice."

"You didn't notice that he left? Can you make that believable?"

"Pretty farfetched, huh?"

"A trifle. Dusty, he's been waiting for quite a while. We can't just ignore the man."

"No, I suppose we can't." Dusty sighed.

"You're sure you wouldn't like to clean up first?"

"I'm sure," Dusty said grimly. Her adolescent urge to giggle at something that wasn't the least bit funny had passed, thank goodness. She stood up straight and squared her shoulders. "Well, here goes."

"Good luck."

"Thanks, I'll probably need it."

Michael heard her coming. He'd been sitting in an overstuffed chair near the fireplace, and he got up slowly as the footsteps got louder.

Dusty stopped in the doorway and didn't even try to put a welcome in her voice. "What a surprise."

His gaze roamed over her. "Hello, Dusty."

With a flick of her eyes, she took in his gray slacks, black loafers and off-white, cable-knit sweater. "You're a long way from home."

Her eyes were as cold as ice, which rubbed him wrong. He should be the cold one, not her. "How've you been?"

Dusty advanced into the room. "Can't complain."

"The ranch looks good."

"I think so."

He was still standing, and she wasn't even hinting that he should sit down. Uncomfortable, Michael moved to the fireplace. "You're different."

"No, I'm exactly the same."

What was wrong? His determination to confront her on that phone call was still with him, but there was something so deadly serious in her eyes, no hint of the woman she'd been in Florida.

One thought was stunning him: Whatever had been developing between him and Dusty in Florida had died a sudden death. For her, anyway. Not for him, although he couldn't pretend to understand the strange woman dodging a direct meeting of their eyes.

"Just passing through?" Dusty questioned flatly.

Right at the moment it seemed prudent to avoid mentioning that his main objective in coming to Wyoming was to see her. "No, actually. I'm looking for a job."

"In Wyoming?"

Her sarcasm stung, but he kept his expression impassive. "Yes, in Wyoming."

"I doubt if you'll find anything around here. In Cheyenne, maybe."

"I'm not looking for something in law."

"Oh?"

"No, I'm all through with that."

"You're *through* with your career?"

"I told you in Florida that things aren't adding up anymore."

"You told me a lot of things in Florida," she muttered.

"Yes, and you told *me* a lot of things."

Dusty's eyes flashed menacingly. "I hope you don't have some weird idea about picking where we left off!"

"Not at all," he lied smoothly, wondering why she was so mad at him. Something was really odd here. Hadn't she gotten his message? Michael's pulse began racing. Hadn't she opened that damned book again?

"My father died," he said abruptly.

Dusty froze and then paled. "Oh, damn. I'm sorry."

She didn't know! She *hadn't* read his note! Why not? What happened after he left that day?

Could he clear the air with a simple explanation?

Something told him no, that Dusty was beyond explanations, simple or otherwise. Recalling her outspoken comments about men and mistakes, Michael's heart sank. That's how Dusty saw him now, as another mistake.

He hadn't expected a hearty welcome after her cold response on the phone, but he honestly hadn't believed that she'd missed reading his message.

His feelings for her hadn't changed. Seeing her, being this close to her, was doing everything to him that he remembered from Florida. He loved her clothes, those worn faded jeans that hugged her long legs and slim hips like a glove, and that sheepskin vest. Her hair was like spun gold, mussed just enough that he would love to untangle it.

He gritted his teeth and shoved his hands into the pockets of his slacks. He was back to square one with Dusty, and it was a deflating conclusion to weeks of uncertainty.

But...he was also back to square one with everything else in his life, and he wasn't going to give up on Dusty any more than he was on his career change. "How about a job?"

She stared, as though he'd suddenly sprouted horns, and echoed numbly, "A job? Here?"

"How many men do you employ?"

She was suddenly very, very wary. "Six, counting Luke, my foreman."

"One of them's quitting."

"How do you know that?"

"He told me. I was out looking around, waiting for you, and I talked to a few of the men. A guy by the name of Lyle is leaving the area, going back to Montana, where he's from."

"Oh, Lyle. Well, yes, but..."

"So, won't that leave you shorthanded?"

"A green hand is worse than none," she snapped.

"Everyone starts out green, Dusty."

"Not on a ranch they don't. Some of those men grew up on ranches."

"And some of them didn't. I can learn, Dusty, the same as you or anyone else."

"Do you even know how to ride a horse?"

"Have you really forgotten the rides we took together that summer?"

Dusty flushed. She'd forgotten nothing. "I'm talking about a range horse."

"Try polo ponies."

Dusty rolled her eyes.

"Don't denigrate something you know nothing about. I can handle any horse you have on the place."

Dusty didn't like the challenge she heard in his voice. "Number one," she said coldly, "I don't believe you know very much about animals. Number two, I don't want to hire a greenhorn. Number three..."

"You're afraid to have me around."

"That's absurd!"

"Maybe, maybe not. I wouldn't have one speck of trouble in dealing with you on an employee-employer basis, but I can't speak for you, can I?"

"I don't believe this! You're a lawyer, not a damned cowboy. Michael, go back to New York. Or go to Cheyenne, if you've suddenly decided to live in Wyoming. But don't ask me for a job. Me, of all people."

He wanted to go to her, to take her in his arms and remind her of that night in Florida.

He stood there and endured her wrath, her incredulity that he would have the gall to reenter her life. Particularly with a request for a job.

"Tell you what," he said calmly, "I'll work without pay for two months. By then I should be able to do a first-rate job."

Dusty really didn't know where to put herself. Compared to Michael, she looked like something that even the cat wouldn't drag in. What had she proved by waltzing in here right off the range, other than that she was capable of taking on a Great-Earth-Mother persona? She smelled like horses, for God's sake.

To make matters worse, Michael was one of those men who didn't just get clean from a shower, he got crisp.

Dusty showed him her back and walked to the large front window. "Why would you want to do menial labor on a ranch?" Her arms were crossed over the front of her bulky vest, and she was wishing to heaven that she'd heeded Nancy's advice to "tidy up" instead of getting first hysterical and then stubborn. "You're educated, you have a profession."

"One I'm not content with."

"That doesn't make any sense."

Michael rubbed his jaw. "I seem to recall my brother saying something to that effect."

Dusty turned. "And coming here, asking *me* for a job... It wouldn't work." She had honestly thought the hurt wouldn't surface, that it was buried so deeply it would never sting again.

But she was feeling it, all of the pain of that day and the subsequent weeks, all over again. How could he come into her home with an innocent face? How could he stand there and pretend that he hadn't inflicted a wound that might never heal? No apologies, not even a hint as to why he had gone off without a word.

Maybe he'd forgotten the whole episode. He had wanted a change of scene and thought of Wyoming, remembering somewhere along the line that he knew a cattle rancher. That was why he was here, the only reason. He was a cad, and worse. He was every woman's nightmare, a man who lied to get what he wanted, who preyed on a woman's weakness for romance and affection and... and love.

Dusty's knees almost gave out, and she reached out to the back of a chair to steady herself. "There are other ranches... hundreds. Go to one of them."

Michael took a few forward steps, his eyes narrowed on her. "Are you all right?"

"I'm fine!" She wasn't fine. She was hurt and embarrassed and terribly humiliated. Never in a million years could she have imagined him just showing up like this. She had tried to forget him and their stupid marriage sixteen years ago and their time together in Florida. She'd steeled herself against memories, both good and bad, and here he was, bringing them all back.

Dusty started from the room. "Please go away. Just...go away."

"Won't you at least think about it? This is where I'd like to work, and you're going to need another hand."

She stopped and took a painfully emotional breath. Was she being unreasonable? After what he did in Florida, could anything she did today be labeled unreasonable?

"Just think about it, Dusty, please. I spotted a little motel about twenty miles back. I'll spend the night there and come back tomorrow."

"Nothing will change in a few hours."

"It might." He was talking to her back again, and he had to stifle an almost overpowering urge to grab her and make her look at him.

But a forceful move now would preclude anything further between them. What had happened to that book? Was it lying around the house somewhere? Dusty was in no mood to listen, but if he had that bookmark in his hands and could show her the message that had obviously eluded her, she would have to believe he'd never meant to hurt her.

"Dusty, I know I took you by surprise today."

"That's putting it mildly." She did turn then, and she even dared to look at his face. Her sliding stomach reaction to his good looks was infuriating, but she was beginning to catch sight of something she had previously thought utterly impossible: revenge.

"Is it all right if I come back tomorrow?"

"Come if you want, but I'm making no promises."

"None expected. Thanks."

"Now . . . if you'll excuse me?"

"Certainly. Don't give it a thought. I can find my own way out."

Believe me, I didn't give it a thought!

By the time Dusty reached her upstairs bedroom, she was shaking like a bowl of gelatin. She peeked through the curtains to see the black Bronco tootling down the driveway.

This was not possible. Michael was *not* in Wyoming!

He'd asked for a job; his father had died. Was there a connection?

Dusty plopped down into a chair, not knowing whether to laugh or cry. She was still trying to decide, when knuckles grazed the door. Nancy came in before the sound had barely registered. "You okay?"

"No."

"You look like hell."

"Thanks, I really needed to hear that."

"You know what I mean. Listen, I was thinking about the way we got so silly in the kitchen. It was nerves."

"I know."

"Oh, you already figured that out."

Dusty pushed herself up and out of the chair. "Well, it certainly wasn't overwhelming elation, Nancy."

Nancy looked sympathetic. "It was pretty bad, huh?"

"It was...unbelievable." Dusty began ripping the heavy-duty snaps open on her vest.

"Did he explain?"

"He explained nothing." Dusty tossed the vest onto the bed. "He never even mentioned that day."

"You're kidding. Well, if he didn't want to talk about that, why did he come?"

"Would you believe a job?"

"A job! What kind of job? I thought you said he was a lawyer."

"He is. He was." Dusty threw up her hands. "I don't know what he is now. I don't know *who* he is now."

"Kind of spooky, if you ask me."

"I should put him to work," Dusty said bitterly. "It would serve him right. A few saddle blisters on his rear end might do him a world of good."

Nancy laughed. "Payback time?"

Dusty hesitated, thinking about the idea, then sighed. "I've never stooped to any such tactics before. I've changed, Nancy."

"I'd say so. You haven't stuck your head out of the house for anything but work since you got back from Florida, and there've been plenty of opportunities." Nancy grinned. "You might as well face it, Dusty, you are always going to attract men."

"Heaven forbid," Dusty muttered with a shudder. The way she felt now, if she never *saw* another man it would be too soon.

But... here was Michael. In Wyoming. Down the road about twenty miles in that fleabag motel, The Mesquite Garden.

Dusty attempted to square her shoulders. If she saw him every day for the rest of her life, she would never mention him leaving Florida. And maybe the only way to get rid of her painful memories was to see him fall off a horse a few times. He was in her world now; *she* had the upper hand.

"I wonder what Luke would think of a complete green-horn in his crew," she said.

"You're considering giving Michael the job? Well, I'm sure Luke will do whatever you want. You are the boss, Dusty."

"But I've always pretty much allowed Luke a free hand with the hiring and firing."

"That's between the two of you. As usual, I intend to stay out of ranch business."

That was true. Nancy had all she could do to keep up with the cooking and housework, which was probably a major factor in the success of the Wilkenses' and Dusty's arrangement. She and Luke ran the ranch; Nancy ran the house. Over the years, the two women had become fast friends, but they might not have become so close if Nancy had inter-fered in Luke and Dusty's working relationship.

"I'd better be getting back to the kitchen," Nancy added. "Whatever you decide, I'm with you."

"Thanks."

The hands all trooped in for supper at six. The men stayed in the bunkhouse but took their meals in the enormous din-ing room in the house. Days off were staggered, so that each man worked five days in a row and then had two off. Ranch chores didn't cease to exist just because the calendar indi-cated that another Saturday or Sunday had arrived, so it was necessary to maintain a seven-day-a-week work crew.

Dusty took her place at the table. She had showered and put on clean clothes, as she did every day for the evening meal, and she wondered, looking at the massive quantities of good food Nancy had prepared, what Michael would be eating for dinner. The nearest café to The Mesquite Garden Motel was nothing to get excited about; rather, it was a place to avoid.

She should be glad he had to order from a greasy menu.

The table talk, as normal, revolved around the chores of the day and the season, interspersed, also as normal, with a lot of good-natured ribbing and laughter. Dusty usually participated, but tonight she subconsciously distanced herself from it all. She found herself pushing the food around on her plate instead of eating with any enjoyment.

Her thoughts were in Florida, back on that beautiful beach, in that little rental house, on the turmoil she had undergone before succumbing to Michael's fatal charm and her own foolish romanticism.

And then on the big night itself, which, regardless of the trauma of the following day, was still the sexual highlight of her life. It had been much more than great lovemaking to her. She was afraid to even get near the word "love," but it lay in the back of her mind like a lead weight, all the same.

She was not over Michael Crowley, not by a long shot. Her feelings had been horribly battered, but they were as much a part of her as the hands at the ends of her arms.

What was she going to do? Having Michael on the ranch would mean sitting down to meals with him, seeing him every single day, talking to him.

But the alternative, refusing him coldly and completely, made the back of her neck feel icy. She rubbed the spot and tried to think of revenge. Wouldn't a little revenge warm up her system? How could she ever make Michael believe how trivial Florida had been if he wasn't within reach?

She visualized herself haughtily walking past him, speaking to him only when necessary, showing him in a hundred small ways how little he meant to her. He would be just another ranch hand, another face at the table, another name on a paycheck.

Not that these men weren't friends. She was normally a friendly person and knew her hired help quite well. Russ, for example, was a widower with two married daughters. Jack spent his evenings with a correspondence course, studying electronics. Bud had an old dog, Dewey, who followed him around the ranch like a second shadow. Lyle was young and lonesome for home, which was why he was leaving at the end of the week. One man was absent, Wyatt, a guy who considered himself pretty smooth with the ladies, and he was probably enjoying his days off with one gal or another.

Then there was Luke, the backbone of the organization. Thank God for Luke Wilkens. Early baldness gave him a long, shiny forehead, and a hint of buckteeth gave him an off-center smile. But Luke Wilkens had a heart of gold and was one of those people whose credo was loyalty and dedication.

And a more loving couple, Luke and Nancy Wilkens, probably couldn't be found in the western hemisphere.

When the men had filed out, Dusty turned to Luke. "Got a few minutes?"

"Sure."

They went to the ranch's office, what had once been a small second parlor in the original design of the decades-old Tremayne house.

Luke folded himself into a chair, but Dusty stalked the room, unable to relax enough to sit down. "I had a visitor today." She wasn't sure what Nancy might have told her husband about Florida, and she wasn't going to ask.

"When I was in Florida I met a man, Michael Crowley. He was from New York City, a lawyer. I had no hint that he might come here, but he did, today. Luke, he wants a job on the ranch."

Luke cleared his throat. "A New York lawyer wants a job on the ranch? Doing what?"

"Not legal research," Dusty replied dryly. "A regular ranch hand. He suggested no pay for two months, a training period."

"Well, that's fair. More than fair."

"It's not the money. What do you think? He's totally green, Luke. He said that he rides and understands horses, but all—*most*—of his experience has been with polo ponies."

"Polo? No kidding? Hey, some of those guys are real riders. Did you ever see a game?"

"No, can't say that I have. Riding well is only part of it, anyway. He's totally ignorant about ranch life."

"Well, everyone's got to start someplace, I suppose. But why'd he come to Wyoming? Wait a minute, did he follow you?" Luke grinned. "Hey, he must have it pretty bad, huh?"

Dusty's face got beet red. "He does not have it bad! There's nothing between us, nothing!"

"Oh." Luke's grin faded.

Dusty could practically see Luke's wheels turning. Her adamant denial had done nothing but make him curious. She felt silly for getting so passionate about his teasing comment.

"Well, it's up to you, Dusty. If you want him working here, then hire 'im. Lyle will be gone by the end of the week, and we'll need to replace him with someone."

"Yes, but with a greenhorn?"

"Crowley being green don't bother me none. If it bothers you, then *don't* hire 'im."

Dusty stood there, a trifle miffed at herself. What had she wanted Luke to do, tell her no way, that he didn't want a greenhorn in his crew?

It would have taken the decision out of her hands, she realized, cleared up this ridiculous mess without her having to make a decision.

"All right, fine. I'll tell him he can have the job," she said flatly.

"Fine." Luke got to his feet. "Anything else?"

"No, nothing else."

"In that case, I'm going out to the kitchen and have another piece of that apple pie. Nancy sure makes good apple pie, don't she?"

"The best," Dusty said absently.

Seven

Michael returned around eight the next morning. Dusty had been staying close to the house, awaiting his arrival. She had deliberately put on old clothes and avoided makeup, ardently hoping that Michael would get the point.

He did, but it wasn't the one Dusty had intended making. Michael thought she looked fantastic, strong and capable and beautiful enough to shake the most levelheaded man. Before this was over, he vowed, looking into her icy eyes, she was going to be a little shook, too. He couldn't be with her and not think about how responsive she'd been to his touch, how uninhibited with her kisses and caresses. She couldn't have just turned those feelings off because of his disappearance, even though it was obvious that she'd tried. He was going to make her admit it, too.

But all in good time.

During a night of dodging lumps in his bed, he'd decided that if Dusty turned him down, he would find a job on another ranch. He was here because of Dusty, unquestionably, but memories of Wyoming and his own personal dissatisfaction in New York had a lot to do with it, too. One thing was certain: He was going to give Wyoming every chance. He'd already taken several large steps and he wasn't turning back now. Tom had been shaken about him leaving the firm, but had finally agreed to buy Michael's interest. Before even seeing Dusty, Michael had purchased the Bronco. His moves, Michael felt, rang of finality.

It was too bad the people he'd stayed with during his seventeenth summer had sold out and left the area years ago, but there were a lot of ranches. He'd find a job, and the closer to the Tremayne spread, the better.

But Dusty surprised him. "You can have the job."

They were standing outside in a wind that was biting enough to put color in Dusty's cheeks. It was March, and anything was possible in Wyoming, even a blizzard.

Michael concealed his elation. "When can I start?"

Dusty looked at his smartly styled, charcoal wool jacket and black kid-leather gloves. "I'd say today, but you're hardly dressed for it."

"Easily solved." Michael grinned. "My things are in the Bronco."

"Fine," Dusty said coolly. "See that brown building off to the left? That's the bunkhouse. There are clean sheets and blankets in one of the closets. Make up a bed for yourself and get settled. Then come to the office in the house and fill out a W-4 form."

A W-4 form was for payroll information, citing an employee's social security number and dependents. He didn't need one yet. "If I'm not drawing pay for two months . . ."

"You'll be drawing pay. No one works on my place without pay."

Michael gritted his teeth. "That wasn't our deal."

"It's *my* deal. Take it or leave it."

Debating the issue would be ridiculous from his standpoint, but Dusty's hard-nosed attitude was tough to swallow. Apparently this was going to be her way or not at all. She was going to make him crawl, if she had to do it by handing him a paycheck he didn't deserve.

She hadn't been so callous sixteen years ago, and she sure hadn't been this way in Florida. Enough was enough.

"Just so you know, the reason I left Florida was because of my father. Tom called. Dad was in the hospital with a heart attack. I left at once. Cora and Mary went with me."

Dusty stared, not immediately able to put it all together. He'd left because of his father? But . . . why hadn't he said so? Even yesterday?

She sucked in an unsteady breath. "I see."

"No, I'm not sure you do. But it's all right. I expect nothing from you because of what happened in Florida. I'm here to work and to learn. For some reason, I don't think I could ever find a better teacher."

Touching his forehead in an informal salute, Michael walked to the Bronco and got in.

The cold wind was making her eyes water. It *was* the wind doing it, wasn't it?

In the next instant hysteria threatened. She stood there, watching the Bronco heading for the bunkhouse, and wished for insensibility.

She got her wish, because her next sensation was an almost numbing emptiness. What *really* had happened in Florida? Even in an emergency situation, couldn't Michael have managed some sort of message? Cora Potter had left one for the gardener, for God's sake!

She felt ill . . . deeply shaken. His story went round and round in her mind.

But his cocky comment about her teaching ability was infuriating. So, he expected nothing from her now? *Yeah, sure.* He wanted to work, to learn? *Tell me another one!*

Dusty turned and started for the house. Maybe he was lying. Maybe he'd gone back to New York, had second thoughts, and decided he wanted another go at her.

She touched her temple. The whole thing was preposterous and giving her a headache. She'd been a fool to trust Michael in Florida, and she was not going to fall into that trap again, no matter how clever he was with mind games.

It would be a lot colder day than this, and in hell, to boot, before she trusted *any* man again.

Going through the house to her office, Dusty was relieved to hear the vacuum cleaner running upstairs. Nancy was busy, which precluded a conversation Dusty wasn't ready to have.

She took off her jacket, dropped it onto a chair and sat at the desk. After a few immobile moments, where she was barely able to think, she got up and dug out a W-4 form from the filing cabinet. Taking it back to the desk, she sat down again.

And realized that she was still too jumpy to think straight. Michael . . . oh, dear God.

She put her elbows on the desk and her face in her hands. Was it true? Had he really received an emergency call from his brother?

It struck her then that she had gone through something very similar to this one other time, when she and Michael had been torn apart by their families. He hadn't contacted her then, either. She'd written dozens of letters and heard nothing from him, not one word.

But he had tried to talk to her this time, and she'd hung up on him.

Dusty groaned. This was like some inane but complex movie plot, with the hero appearing and disappearing every sixteen years. Why was it happening to her?

At the sound of footsteps on the first floor of the house, Dusty lowered her hands and sat up straight. Michael appeared in the doorway. He was wearing jeans, boots, a plain blue shirt and a denim jacket. There was a tan felt hat in his hand.

"Got that form for me?"

"Yes." Dusty picked it up. "It'll only take a minute to fill out."

Michael crossed to the desk and took the form from her. "Got a pen?"

"Right here." Dusty handed him a ballpoint.

"Thanks." There was a chair at the front of the desk, and Michael sat down to tend to the W-4.

With his head bent forward, Dusty was free to stare. Michael looked different in those clothes, more like Luke and the other hands. Not at all like a New York lawyer. Why would a man with his education and profession want to be a cowboy?

Shaking her head, she rubbed her aching forehead with her fingertips. Thinking she understood men seemed embarrassingly arrogant. She understood nothing, not about men, not about women, certainly not about relationships.

Michael looked up. "All done. What's next?"

"You go to work." Dusty got to her feet. "It's calving season. The cows have been isolated in a pasture just south of the river. That's where Luke and the men are. Saddle a horse and ride out there. Luke will tell you what to do."

Michael stood up. "Any particular horse?"

"Any one of them that strikes your fancy...and you can catch."

"And the saddle?"

"In the tack room, which you'll find in the smallest barn. Just for future reference, Luke will be your teacher, not me."

Michael looked her up and down. "That's probably best. I'm not here to get in your hair."

Like hell you're not! Dusty regarded him coolly. "Of course not."

Michael walked to the door. "By the way, that book you were reading in Florida? What did you do with it?"

Dusty's already-strained mind went blank. "What book?"

"I saw it several times. It had a bright red cover."

"Do you want to read it?" Dusty was trying to figure out which book he was talking about. She'd had several with her, but she'd been reading...or attempting to read...

It came to her suddenly. "The one with a red cover is a historical romance. Are you interested in historical romances?'' she asked dryly. Would this man never cease startling her?

Michael couldn't help laughing. "That strikes you as funny, doesn't it?"

"Hilarious," Dusty replied mirthlessly.

"Well, funny or not, I'm an avid reader of—" Michael cleared his throat "—historical romances. That one looked particularly...uh...spicy. Do you have it?"

"It wasn't spicy and it wasn't good. I never finished it."

The last piece of the puzzle fell into place for Michael. Dusty hadn't so much as opened the book again. "But you have it?"

"I have no idea."

"If you run across it . . ."

"I'll save it for you." Was he pulling her leg? He was an avid reader of historical romances? *Come on.*

Nancy stuck her head in. "Oh, sorry."

"Nancy Wilkens, Michael Crowley," Dusty recited tonelessly.

Nancy smiled. "Yes, we introduced ourselves yesterday. Looks like you're all ready to go to work, Michael."

"I'm legal, at any rate."

"Legal?"

"He just filled out a W-4," Dusty clarified.

"Oh, but I thought..." Nancy stammered.

"So did I," Michael drawled. He stuck the tan hat on his head. "Well, do I look like a cowboy?"

"You look—" Dusty stopped herself just short of saying "silly." It would be a lie, anyway. Michael might look different than he did in the excellent clothes she'd seen him wear, but he didn't look silly.

In fact, he looked so handsome in his Western garb that Dusty found herself clenching her teeth.

"Luke's expecting you," she reminded glumly.

Michael grinned. "Sure thing, boss. See you later, Nancy."

"At supper," Nancy said cheerily. "Luke has lunch for everyone with him."

When Michael was gone, Dusty sank behind the desk. She hated being called "boss." Groaning aloud, she put her head down on it.

"Is it really that bad?"

Dusty raised her head. "It's worse."

"He seems like a very nice guy, Dusty."

"That's what he wants everyone—*women*—to think."

Nancy's eyes widened. "Really?"

Dusty groaned again and held her head. "I don't know. I don't know anything about anything."

"Well, I do." Nancy perched on the chair Michael had used. "Michael Crowley is here for only one reason. You. Something serious must have happened to pull him out of Florida. Hasn't he explained it?"

Dusty put her throbbing head back against the chair and closed her eyes. "He...tried. I'm trying to decide if I should believe him."

"And you'd rather not discuss it."

"Maybe later." Dusty's eyes opened enough to see her friend. "Do you mind?"

"Of course not. If you want to talk about it, I'm here."

"Thanks, Nancy." Dusty listened to her friend leaving the office, and the subsequent silence felt good, almost peaceful.

Almost. She never should have given Michael a job, not if peace was what she wanted.

What in heaven's name was behind his gibberish about that dumb book? Michael didn't read historical romances. She'd bet the ranch on that.

It made as much sense as everything else going on, Dusty thought with a dejected sigh. If she wasn't so torn up where Michael was concerned, she would sit him down and pick his brain. Really get to the bottom of things. She'd know if he was lying with an in-depth question-and-answer session. If he'd cooperate, of course.

She wasn't up to it, though. Her Florida wounds hadn't healed, even if the story he'd related today was meticulously accurate and she had overreacted that morning.

Maybe the damage wasn't all Michael's doing. She'd been particularly vulnerable with those stupid decisions racking her in that rental house. But how many times was she destined to go through these ups and downs with men?

She didn't want any more complications in the name of romance. She was thirty-three years old and weary of the game. Whatever was in Michael's mind about working on the Tremayne ranch—obviously to put the two of them in proximity—he was in for a rude awakening: She was having no part of it.

He would get the message eventually and be on his way, it was as simple as that.

In the meanwhile, she had work to do. Her major chore for the day was a trip to Casper to do some banking and fill a shopping list, which included groceries and a part for one of the tractors that had broken down. She had best get started.

Dusty got back from Casper around four. She'd taken one of the ranch's pickup trucks and returned with its bed loaded. There were boxes of food, cases of motor oil, a packet containing serum to inoculate the new calves, and the part for the tractor. It took nearly an hour to unload and distribute her purchases.

After a few words with Nancy about the long day of errands, Dusty went upstairs for a shower. She hadn't been able to avoid thinking about Michael while she tended to business, and she suspected she might never see his presence on the ranch as ordinary. His being in this part of Wyoming at all wasn't ordinary, but his working on the ranch was unbelievable. Even though she'd given him the job herself.

At six, four of the men came in for supper—Luke, Russ, Lyle and Michael. The others, Luke stated, were with the cows. "Lots of births today. We're going back to keep an eye on things after we eat, then the others can come for supper. Is that okay, honey?" he said to Nancy.

"Of course," Nancy said agreeably, not at all bothered that she would be serving two separate meals. Luke strongly believed in preventive medicine with the animals, and he'd saved many a calf's life by being present to help out with a difficult birth.

Dusty took her place at the table, noting that Michael looked tired but seemed to be as comfortable as a pair of old jeans. After a brief "hello" he barely looked at her, certainly no more than the other hungry hands did. They passed platters and bowls and dived into the food as though their last meal had been days ago.

Hungry herself, Dusty did justice to Nancy's delicious pot roast and freshly baked bread. Comments and sporadic discussions of the day's work accompanied the meal, but it was well underway when Dusty heard something from Russ that widened her eyes.

"You sure you've never played midwife with cattle before, Mac?"

Mac? Michael answered, so Russ must be talking to him. But, "Mac"? Not "Mike," which might be expected—Mac.

Dusty lowered her fork, gave Michael a good hard stare and said wryly, "Please pass the salt down to this end of the table, *Mac.*"

Michael laughed and reached for the saltshaker. "Here you go, boss."

Luke snickered, Nancy giggled, and Russ and Lyle grinned. Dusty gave them all an exaggerated sweet smile. "If anyone calls me 'boss' again, I'll dump my pot roast over his head."

The table broke up, with Dusty laughing as heartily as the others. Still, no one called her "boss" again.

The men didn't linger at the table, as they usually did at the evening meal. Rather, they finished quickly and left to relieve those who'd stayed with the cows.

The dining room was silent with the men gone. Nancy got up to put the meat and vegetables into the oven to stay warm, but Dusty barely moved. Apparently Nancy sensed her friend's unsettled mood, because she returned to the table with a comforting, "He's doing fine, Dusty."

Dusty smiled humorlessly. "He's getting an education, with his first day being right at the height of calving."

"He may as well learn what it's all about from the onset."

"True."

True or not, Michael's tired face remained in Dusty's mind. He wasn't used to doing physical labor, and it annoyed her that he was trying.

It was also annoying that he'd barely said hello and then only spoken to her during the meal with that snide "boss" remark.

Of course, she'd asked for it. Her pronunciation of "Mac" had hardly been flattering.

But he wasn't a Mac, he was a Michael!

"The men will probably sleep in shifts tonight," Nancy remarked.

"More than likely," Dusty agreed, although she was really thinking, rather grumpily, about Michael fitting in so well. She hadn't thought he would. Actually she'd envisioned him as being more of a sore thumb than any real help out in the birthing pasture. Apparently he'd already earned Russ's respect, which was no small feat. The older man had cowboyed his whole life and wasn't quick to hand out compliments to greenhorns.

That night, after Dusty turned off the lights in her bedroom, she stood at the window and looked at the distant dark shape of the bunkhouse. Several yard lights illuminated circular patches of the compound. The March wind whipped barren tree limbs into eerie dances. A dim light burned in the barn.

Luke was still out with the cows; Nancy had gone to bed. Everything was quiet, but some of the men were with Luke. Michael could be in the bunkhouse or still working. It bothered Dusty to place him out in that cold, dark pasture, working with flashlights and lanterns. His first day as a ranch hand just might be his last. If he had an ounce of sense, that is.

Dusty wasn't alone. Nancy was just down the hall, and some of the men were in the bunkhouse. It was a rare occasion for Dusty to be completely alone on the ranch, but that's how she felt, alone and painfully lonely.

It was the dark night, she decided uneasily, the wind-tossed trees. The ranch was miles from its nearest neighbor, a factor that ordinarily was a very big plus for Dusty.

Tonight it wasn't. Tonight she would like to look out the window and see the lights and population of a town. A city. Hear car horns blaring, traffic noises. If she went outside she would be able to pick up sounds from the pastures, but none was strong enough to penetrate the sturdy walls of the house.

Shivering, Dusty left the window and crawled into bed. Michael's being on the ranch had changed everything. When word got around that she'd come home from her vacation, friends had called. She had turned down every invitation, and lately she was getting fewer calls.

Now this, being uncomfortable because of a dark night and a little wind. It was all Michael's doing, every single drop of her discomfort and self-imposed exile from friends and activities.

Dammit, what was he doing here? He didn't belong in a dark pasture bringing calves into the world! He'd probably end up injured. Or worse. He didn't know his way around a ranch, and she'd been a damned fool to give him a job. If he did get hurt, it would be her fault.

It was two hours later when she heard Luke coming up the stairs. She was still awake, still worrying, still cussing Michael, and herself.

She jumped out of bed, grabbed a robe and intercepted Luke just before he went into his and Nancy's room. "Luke!"

He stopped with his hand on the doorknob. "You still awake?"

Dusty tied the sash of her bathrobe. "How'd it go?"

"About normal. No major calamities, at least. How come you're still awake?"

"Just restless. Luke . . . how did Michael do?"

"He did all right."

"Oh. Well, I was wondering . . ."

"He's a worker, willing to tackle anything." Luke tried to stifle a yawn.

"Go on to bed," Dusty said. "You look ready to drop."

"I'm a little tired, all right. See ya in the morning."

"Good night, Luke. And thanks."

"Get some sleep, Dusty. You don't have to worry about Michael. He'll work out just fine."

"If . . . he stays."

"He'll stay. Night, Dusty."

Dusty slowly walked to her bedroom, went in and quietly closed the door. For some strange reason she felt calmer, more prepared for sleep.

Maybe she'd only needed to hear that Michael had survived his first day as a cowboy.

Eight

In the next few days Dusty rode out to the river pasture several times, ostensibly to see for herself how the cows and newborn calves were doing.

But she was trying not to lie to herself about Michael, and deep inside she had to admit that she was a lot more interested in how *he* was doing.

He always nodded to her, or if close enough, said "Hi, how are you?" But that was it. Beyond the evening meal, which was the gathering time of day for the people on the ranch, Dusty did little more than catch glimpses of Michael. He made no effort to speak to her alone, which began to grate on her nerves. Not that she wanted him to seek her out; if he did, she wouldn't like it.

But the fact that he didn't, irritated her, which, she told herself wryly, was certainly a mature attitude. Mature or not, he seemed perfectly comfortable with the arrangement and she was not. She wasn't lying awake every night, as she had after his first day on the job, but the situation was a constant burr, nonetheless.

It boiled down to a simple fact: She regretted giving Michael a job and had no solid, sensible reason for canceling the arrangement. She couldn't just fire him, not without cause, and she felt herself locked into the distressing situation.

Neither Luke nor Nancy knew about Dusty's first hastily aborted marriage. Very few people knew about it. Racking her brain, Dusty tried to think of who might have been told at the time and would remember the episode distinctly enough to make a connection between it and today's Michael Crowley. Her conclusion was comforting: Anyone who was aware of the unpublicized marriage no longer lived in the area, specifically, her ex-husband, Trent, and the girl who'd been her best friend in high school.

She was in the barn one afternoon, puttering with various small tasks and debating the question of whether she should tell Nancy about her and Michael's past, when Lyle came in. "Can I talk to you for a minute, Dusty?"

"Sure. What's up?" Lyle was scheduled to leave for good in another day. He was nineteen and looked younger, and Dusty understood his longing for home. He had no more than a dozen whiskers on his chin, and he blushed easily, a pink-cheeked boy, even with years of ranch experience behind him.

"Uh...would it be all right if I stayed on for another couple of weeks?"

The question surprised Dusty. "Well...I don't know, Lyle. Why do you want to stay? I thought you were anxious to get back to Montana?"

Lyle shifted his feet and got red in the face. "I'm not goin' home alone, Dusty. There's a girl...we're gonna get married...but she can't leave for another two weeks. Some kind of mix-up with her job. Anyways, I'd sure like to stay on until Deb...that's her name...she don't wanna leave her job without references...is free to leave."

"Young love" was looking Dusty right in the face. She sighed softly and thought of her and Michael and that wonderful, sad summer.

Lyle's staying wasn't financially best for her. Michael had been given the boy's job, even though their employment had overlapped by a few days.

But, looking at Lyle's youthful features, Dusty knew she couldn't refuse his request. Besides, it was calving season, and Luke would probably welcome an extra hand for a few weeks.

"Yes," she said. "It's all right with me. Have you talked to Luke about it?"

"Mentioned it, but he said to talk to you."

"I'll pass my okay on to Luke." Dusty smiled. "Congratulations. I hope you and Deb will be very happy."

Lyle's face got redder. "Thanks. I better be gettin' back to work."

Michael and Lyle looked nothing alike, but the boy reminded Dusty of Michael at seventeen. There was something very special about first love, although the two years between seventeen and nineteen were monumental. Deb and Lyle were self-supporting, Dusty and Michael hadn't been. Pragmatically, Dusty knew that she and Michael getting married so young had been a foolish move. She had to question how long their marriage would have lasted if no one had intervened.

But she couldn't question their feelings for each other that summer, particularly her own. Her love for Michael had been as real as anything she had ever experienced.

Dusty walked out of the barn. Lyle was gone and the compound was vacant. She was dressed in warm clothes. The temperature was chilly, with an overcast sky and a nipping wind. Television weathermen kept forcasting storms, but none had developed in the immediate area.

With the distant past so strong in her mind, Dusty felt an urge to find Michael and talk about Florida. The memory of their lovemaking made her breath catch and her heart beat faster.

Immediately, though, doubts began plaguing her. He'd gone off without a word, regardless of how dire the situation in New York. Cora had gone with him and had found the time to scribble a note to her gardener, so Michael's silence wasn't because of a tight schedule. He had, more than likely, simply forgotten she existed.

Dusty had been trying to look at it fairly. Hearing that his father was in the hospital with a serious heart attack had to have been stressful. But Dusty had been through two stressful episodes with her own parents and hadn't forgotten everything else in the process. She knew, without question, that if the situation in Florida had been reversed and she'd been the one called away by an emergency, she would have found some way to notify Michael. She could come up with several different options. A note on the door seemed the most logical, but if nothing else, Michael could have told a third party—one of the neighbors, perhaps—who would pass it on.

It just seemed very coldhearted that he'd made love with her at night and then completely forgotten her in the morning, regardless of circumstances. She would never have done that to him.

Dusty sighed and began slowly walking toward the house. She and Michael were adults and responsible for their own actions. Maybe he'd thought about that in New York and was sorry he'd behaved so thoughtlessly. Maybe he'd really come to the ranch to apologize.

The *maybes* stacked up but didn't make Dusty feel much better. Michael working for her was ridiculous. She hated him being called ''Mac'' by the men, which was nothing to get upset about but was consistently annoying.

Michael didn't know the ropes of ranching or the country. She couldn't go to Luke and ask him to keep a protective eye on one particular man, Luke had enough to do. But worrying about Michael getting hurt was a gnawing intrusion on her own work.

As for telling Nancy the whole story, she probably should. She probably *would* . . . one of these days.

Almost a week later, while doing the semimonthly payroll, Dusty became very still. At her desk in the office, she studied Michael's time sheet. All of the other hired hands had worked their five days and taken two off, but Michael had been on the job every single day since he began.

Unaccustomed anger sliced through her. Michael had no right to make his own rules.

The calving was slowing down, and Dusty knew that Luke had some of the men doing other chores. Where she might find Michael was anybody's guess, but she intended to lay down the law to him. Grabbing her jacket and hat, she tore through the house and exited by the back door.

The fresh, cold air cleared her head. She didn't ordinarily go around Luke to deal with the men, and this was not the incident to change a long-standing routine.

Dusty found Luke at the equipment shed, where he was checking over the swather, a machine used during haying. He looked up. "Hi."

"Hi. Luke, I'm doing the payroll. Michael hasn't taken any time off."

Luke straightened up from the swather and picked up a rag to wipe the grease off his hands. "He said he'd rather work."

"That's not his decision."

"I told him you wouldn't like it, but he said he didn't have anything better to do."

"He could rest!" Dusty waved her hand. "He could see the country or... or go to Casper or any number of places!"

Luke shrugged. "Can't make a man go sight-seeing if he don't wanna go, Dusty."

"That's not the point." Dusty was fuming, which was unusual for her. If Michael was in reach right now, she'd tell him a thing or two. "Where's he working today?"

"Him and Bud are clearing snags out of High Pass."

Pass Creek went by two names, High Pass and Low Pass, depending on which section of the creek one was referring to. Michael pulling snags—tree limbs and branches brought down by the melting snow—out of High Pass placed him in the mountains, but High Pass wound up and down for many miles.

She would have to wait until this evening to talk to him, which, when she thought about it, was undoubtedly best. Her mood was just barely friendly, and she'd prefer talking to Michael at a calmer moment.

With effort she managed to turn her thoughts. "Is there a problem with the swather?"

"Just making a few minor repairs," Luke assured her.

Michael's skin was getting ruddy from the raw weather, Dusty noted when he came to the office that evening. "This shouldn't take long," she said evenly. "Please sit down."

He lowered himself to the chair at the front of the desk and grinned faintly. "Am I getting the ax?"

It startled her that he would think he was going to be fired just because she had asked him to stop at the office before leaving the house after supper. Perhaps he'd been sensing her tension.

Dusty maintained an impassive expression. "You're not getting the ax, but I do have something to say."

"Figured you did."

"You know what it's about, too, don't you?"

"I've got an idea."

Dusty looked at him across the desk. He was too good-looking for her comfort. This evening his shirt was a blue-gray wool blend, and its smooth lines hugged his broad shoulders—which seemed to be getting broader—and his chest. Her own sensual nature worked against her with Michael. He was sitting casually, one arm hooked over a corner of the chair back, but everything about him boldly announced, *I'm a man, you're a woman!*

"Um . . . you have to take time off," she stated, striving for a businesslike manner.

"Why?"

Dusty recovered some composure. "With your law background, you have to know something about labor laws."

"Never really got into that field, but I seem to recall that the law is more lenient with farm labor."

"Yes, it is, but ranch policy . . ."

"Luke works nonstop."

"Luke is not the issue."

"Guess not." Michael looked directly into her eyes. "You don't like me working here, do you?"

It was the perfect opening for brutal honesty, for telling him flat-out how she felt. Instead of doing so, Dusty said rather sharply, "I suppose *you* like it?"

"Yes, as a matter of fact, I do."

"Don't you find it odd? You working for me?"

"Maybe I'm missing something, but no, it doesn't seem at all odd to me." Michael thoughtfully regarded her through a silent stretch. Her sweater was pink and bulky; he'd noticed it at supper. Her hair shone from the overhead light, and he easily recalled its arousing scent and texture. Her eyes, as striking as they were, were completely unreadable.

"What do you want me to do, Dusty?"

"I want you to—" Dusty stopped before she blurted, *to go back to New York.* Then she continued. "I want you to take regular days off, like everyone else." In the next instant she realized with a sinking sensation that she didn't want him leaving entirely. She only wanted him to... to...

She honestly didn't know *what* she wanted from Michael, and the knowledge wasn't at all soothing.

Michael got up and walked around the room. Standing and moving, his presence was more formidable to Dusty. She tried not to look at his long legs and firm behind, but her gaze kept betraying her.

She drew a breath. "Your taking regular days off is not an unreasonable request."

"No, it's not." Michael stopped at a bookcase and scanned the paperbacks. Smiling suddenly, he pulled out one with a brilliant red cover. "Is this the book you were reading in Florida?"

Good grief, thought Dusty. Was he back on that stupid book?

Michael fanned the pages and frowned. There was no bookmark. He turned to face Dusty and held up the book. "Is this the one?"

Disgruntled, Dusty stood up and walked over to him. "Let me see it." She took the book from his hand. "No, this one's over a year old. The one you saw was new."

Relief flooded Michael's system, and he quickly checked the other books on the shelves. None, other than the one Dusty was holding, had a cover of the color he remembered.

"But, please," Dusty drawled dryly. "Take this one, if you're dying to read a historical romance. In fact, help yourself. There must be a dozen of them in this case."

There were all kinds of books in the case, but not too many that Michael would enjoy reading. His little charade struck him as funny and he laughed softly. "Thanks, I'll take the red one."

"Got a thing for paperbacks with red covers?"

If he had a "thing," it was for the lady holding the paperback. He'd like to tell her so, too, and one of these days, he would.

But she wasn't over the Florida fiasco yet. Her attitude spoke clearly of unforgotten and certainly unforgiven hurt. The time would come, he sincerely believed, when Dusty would be less cool, when the woman he'd made love with in Florida would emerge again. In the meantime, he was working and learning, and the discovery that he had a genuine affinity with animals and the land was elating.

Dusty held the book out, intending to pass it to him, although the image of him actually reading it was discombobulating. Their hands touched, and Michael did nothing to hurry the process.

Dusty, however, hurried so much the book tumbled to the floor. They both stooped to get it and their heads collided.

"Ouch!" Dusty cried, and fell back on her seat.

Michael plopped down on the carpet and rubbed his forehead. "One of us has an awfully hard head."

Dusty began scrambling to her feet. "Yes, and we know *which* one, don't we?"

The red paperback was on the floor, forgotten. Michael put his hands on Dusty's shoulders and stopped her from rising. "Are you talking about me?"

She glared into his amused face. "If the shoe fits..."

He looked back, and their gazes melded. His eyes were a deep, dark blue, radiating admiration. Dusty couldn't dilute the value of sexual desire in anyone. Without sex, the world would be a very dull place, indeed. Michael's desire was apparent in his touch, his eyes; hers had begun broiling within her.

In an instant she was back in that little rental house on the beach, torn, ambivalent, but unable to halt the rushing tide that had brought her and Michael together. Emotions churned within her, breathlessness threatened.

"Ahh," Michael murmured, deeply affected by what he was seeing in Dusty's eyes. He lowered his head, slowly, and moved his hands from her shoulders to her face. "Dusty," he whispered.

He was going to kiss her. Slightly dazed, Dusty parted her lips. A kiss...yes. His mouth on hers. His hands were heating her face. She could feel his warm breath, smell his after-shave. Her heart was pounding.

But one kiss wouldn't do it for either of them.

She pulled away abruptly and shook off his hands. He sat back until she was on her feet, then got up from the floor himself.

Smoothing her hair, Dusty started for the desk. Halfway, she spun around. "Let's get something straight. I won't be mauled...not by anyone."

Michael raised an eyebrow. "'Mauled' seems like a rather strong word."

"Call it whatever you like, but don't try anything again." Dusty watched him lean against the bookcase, slouching carelessly in a pose she never would have thought him capable of striking. Damn, he was handsome!

"Should I assume, in that case," Michael said softly, "that I should wait for you to do the mauling?"

Dusty stiffened. "Don't hold your breath!"

"You'd like to jump my bones this very minute."

"I most certainly would not!" Flustered, Dusty whirled around without direction. "This is getting out of hand. Look, if that's what's on your mind, maybe you'd better find another place to live."

"And work?"

There was a standoff in the air, fragile in its newness, nearly lethal in its intensity. Dusty's breath caught and held. Here was a second chance to rid herself of this man once and for all, another perfect opening.

She became very nervous, with her eyes darting around the room then back to Michael. He was different, dammit, *different!* At seventeen he'd been sweet, in Florida he'd been incredibly sexy, now he was...what? Less than two weeks in Wyoming couldn't have toughened him, could it?

No, it wasn't that he was so tough, it was that he was determined. Yes, that was it: Michael was as resolute as anyone she'd ever seen.

But so was she. Dusty's shoulders lifted and went back, her chin up. "We made a deal on your working here. Whether you stick with it or not is up to you."

"Oh, I'll stick, never fear."

"But you'll abide by the existing rules."

Michael grinned, insolently, Dusty felt. "Yes, I'll abide."

"Your first two days off start in the morning," she said in a tone that dared him to disagree.

"Fine." Michael pushed away from the bookcase. "I'll sleep in tomorrow." He bent over and scooped up the red-covered paperback, studied it for a moment, then raised his eyes to Dusty. "Looks promising. I'll let you know how I like it."

Dusty rolled her eyes. "I'll await the news with bated breath."

Michael couldn't help laughing, and received a curious, narrow-eyed look from Dusty because of it. He cleared his throat. "Well, I suppose this conference is over."

For one fleeting moment, the idea of him staying and talking about something important slowed Dusty's responses.

"Unless..." Michael said speculatively.

"No," Dusty said quickly. "It's over. Good night." She proceeded to the desk and sat down.

Michael walked to the doorway without haste, where he paused. "By the way, I really like that pink sweater."

Dusty's lips barely moved. "Thanks."

Starting out, Michael hesitated again. "I don't suppose you'd care to go somewhere with me tomorrow. We could just wander around, maybe have dinner in Casper, a movie afterward."

"Bad idea."

"Yeah, I thought you'd say something like that." Michael grinned. "Can't blame a guy for trying. See ya around."

How casual he sounded, how nonplussed! Dusty stared at the vacant doorway. Uncertainty arose, doubt that she was the stronger. When had Michael become so invincible? Or... was the Wyoming life-style intensifying qualities he'd already possessed? After all, did she really know him? A few days in the Florida sun and one night of moonlight was not enough time together, dramatic as it had been, for any real knowledge to develop. Wasn't she the one who believed a man's true colors didn't surface until the flames had died down, anyway?

Their flames weren't even close to dying. If he'd kissed her when they'd been on the floor, anything might have happened.

Putting her elbows on the desk, Dusty clasped her hands and rested her chin on them with a troubled expression. Michael was stronger—*tougher*—than she'd believed. Intermingled with his resolve was a streak of toughness she hadn't detected in Florida. Maybe it had been completely apparent and she'd missed it in light of more personally disturbing elements.

Whatever, there were facets to his personality she hadn't gotten near. But did resolve and even toughness guarantee safety in this rugged, only partially tamed country? Somewhere along the line, people living in barely populated areas, such as where the Tremayne ranch was located, gained a sort of sixth sense. They automatically watched for rattlers and gopher holes, and they knew what to expect from animals, both domestic and wild.

Michael was a city man. Granted, he looked fantastic in jeans and boots, but looking like the epitome of Western man did not make him a cowboy.

At least Luke wasn't sending him off by himself yet, thank God. Today he'd paired Michael with Bud for that jaunt to High Pass. Dusty shivered at the thought of Michael running into a grizzly bear in the mountains. Grizzlies had once roamed the prairie, but civilization had gradually driven the unpredictable animals to higher ground.

Not that grizzlies were a major problem, but they were sighted every so often, and Dusty had heard plenty of frightening tales about encounters with the huge bears.

She sighed. Worrying about Michael running into a grizzly was reaching. Her true concern was focused more on everyday routine—a slipped or broken cinch belt, a fall from a horse—and it was probably silly, at that, because very few hired men had been injured on the Tremayne ranch.

But they'd all been seasoned hands, and Michael was a greenhorn, determined to succeed or not.

Why did he want to do it? Was she the big draw? Yes, he'd talked about dissatisfaction with his career, but why Wyoming? Why become a cowboy?

The most profound question of all appeared again and stayed in her mind: Why had he been so blasé about their burgeoning relationship in Florida and then traveled such a long distance to intrude on her life?

Dusty was still pondering when Nancy stuck her head in. "Still working?"

"No, just thinking."

"I'm going up to bed. Luke went out. Need anything?"

"Luke went out?" Dusty stood up. "How come?"

"Checking on the new mamas. He said he wouldn't be long."

"Mares or cows?"

"The mares. He went down to the barn."

Three mares had delivered in the past week and there were eleven more due to foal. The horses were pastured much closer to the house than the cattle, and when a mare's time got close, she was moved into the barn. Luke was such an old hand at delivering babies, Dusty usually stayed out of it.

Tonight she was too restless to go to bed. "I don't need anything, Nancy, you go on to bed. I think I'll go see what's happening in the barn."

"All right. See you in the morning."

"Good night, Nancy."

"Night, Dusty."

Nine

Dusty didn't see Michael or his vehicle for the next two days. She caught herself watching for both and wondering what Michael had found to occupy himself so thoroughly that he didn't even return to the ranch at night. A woman was the logical answer. Michael was young and healthy, and with his looks he'd have no problem at all in finding a willing female.

Dread made Dusty's pulse quicken, but, she told herself sternly, if he was that fickle more power to him. Let him line up women, let him have a new one every week. Did she care what he did?

It was a self-protective reaction, of course, nothing more. She *did* care what he did, and not merely from an employer's standpoint, or even out of friendship. She and Michael could never be mere friends; there'd been too much between them to pretend nothing out of the ordinary had happened.

At moments Dusty became weak-kneed from memory. Twice in her life she'd been positive that she was in love with

Michael Crowley, not once, dammit, twice! At seventeen her excuse had been bone-deep sincerity and naiveté, at thirty-three, she'd been merely stupid. *Easy* was an even better word: In Florida she'd been disgustingly easy.

The years between seventeen and thirty-three hadn't been any great shakes, either. The men she'd known had been takers, and she'd been so damned willing to give. The whole concept of male-female relationships was exasperating, frustrating. Maybe the women who played by men's rules were the best off.

Dusty recognized cynicism in herself, which angered her. Before Florida, she had at least escaped that unflattering quality. Michael's desertion, however sound its cause, had been a final straw. One word from him that morning would have been enough, just some small sign that he'd thought of her, remembered her. Maybe what was most painful about that night was its resemblance to a tasteless, loveless, quickie affair, and she had prided herself on avoiding such encounters. That bit of pride, which had always given Dusty a modicum of self-satisfaction, had been virtually destroyed.

Bottom line: If Michael had not come to Wyoming, she would have relegated him to her private list of mistakes and tried very hard to forget the whole episode; his presence was no reason to change attitudes.

Still, when his Bronco drove into the compound in the late afternoon of his second free day, Dusty suffered a choking sensation. Standing near the corral, where Luke, Wyatt and Jack were discussing the upcoming chore of breaking last year's foals, Dusty's entire system focused on that returning Bronco. The vehicle progressed at a slow speed and finally stopped near the bunkhouse.

Watching out of the corner of her eye, Dusty saw Michael climb from behind the wheel and stretch himself. His arms went up and he wriggled his back, as though he'd been sitting for a long time. Jeans and shirt tautened, delineating maleness, and Dusty felt jarred by the view.

The three men standing nearby maintained their conversation, although Dusty saw that they, too, were aware of Michael's arrival.

Michael closed the door of the Bronco and began ambling their way. Luke, Jack and Wyatt all said hello, with Wyatt immediately making cracks about Michael's activities for the past two days. Wyatt was consistent, Dusty thought dryly. The man thought of little else beyond women, although he was a first-rate cowhand.

Wyatt's jibes didn't appear to affect Michael much. He turned and smiled at Dusty. "Hi."

"Hello, Michael."

Michael announced to the party at large, "I've been at Cody. What a great place!"

"Sure is," Wyatt agreed and looked at Dusty. His expression stated clearly that her presence was a deterrent to one of those man-to-man stories about women.

She stood her ground; they could talk about wine, women and song at another time.

"Did you see the Buffalo Bill Historical Center?" she asked Michael.

"Spent about six hours in it. Wonderful Western art collection."

Wyatt looked pained, but it pleased Dusty that Michael had done more than goof off during his reprieve from the daily grind, and she gave Wyatt a rather triumphant glance while asking Michael, "Did you drive through Thermopolis, by any chance?"

They all talked about the massive hot springs at the town of Thermopolis, which Michael declared had to be the West's best-kept secret. "I'd never even heard about it before, and that mineral hot spring is the largest in the world. It's amazing."

After a few minutes, Luke and the other two men drifted away. Michael leaned on the corral fence. "Wyoming is incredible, Dusty. I drove through beautiful country in the past two days. The Wind River Canyon is spectacular. I'm planning on another visit to Thermopolis and Cody."

"Did you stop at any of the small town museums? Some of them are marvelous, Michael. Full of old things, photographs, household articles, even clothing."

For several minutes they discussed local attractions. While they talked, Dusty felt something relenting within her. For the first time since Michael's surprising arrival in Wyoming, she was speaking to him without bitterness.

"Too bad the weather wasn't a little better for your first tour," she commented. The sky had been overcast and threatening all during Michael's absence.

"The weather's fine, Dusty. Only one thing would have made my tour better." He smiled. "But maybe I'd better not get into that."

The five-minute dinner bell rang, which was really a warning that Nancy was putting the hot food on the table. The men began walking to the house, coming from different directions.

"You haven't eaten, have you?" Dusty said, ignoring the pronounced thrill she'd received from Michael's gentle flirting.

"No, I've been driving all afternoon."

"Then you must be hungry. Shall we go in to supper?"

"Yes, thanks."

The wind woke Dusty around one a.m. that night. She lay in bed with the blankets tucked around her and listened to the mournful wailing outside. Strong gusts were hitting the house hard enough to rattle the windowpanes; it was coming from the north. If that long-promised storm didn't break by morning, she'd be surprised.

She drifted off and was awakened again at four by the telephone. Luke was already answering when Dusty picked up her bedroom extension.

"Luke? This is Deputy Joe Rawlins. You've got cattle on the highway. Wind must have knocked down a fence."

"Hell! Tell me where, Joe."

Dusty listened to the location, then spoke up. "Luke, that's near the bulls' pasture."

"Sure is," Luke said. "Did you see the cattle yourself, Joe?"

"No. Whoever called in just said 'cattle.' Could be bulls, I suppose."

"We'll get right out there, Joe. Thanks for calling."

"Thanks, Joe," Dusty said and put the phone down. She moved quickly then, getting out of bed and scrambling into her clothes. The wind was still howling, but she didn't hear any rain.

She and Luke reached the kitchen at the same time. "I'm going out to wake the men, Dusty. If the bulls are out, this could take some doing."

"We'd better bring horses with us, Luke. The animals might have wandered away from the road."

"Good idea."

Nancy came in, tying her robe. "I'll make coffee and fix some thermos jugs."

"Thanks, honey." Luke kissed his wife's cheek and turned to Dusty. "Do you wanna wait for the coffee? It'd give the men a chance to get dressed."

"I'll wait," Dusty agreed. Nancy was already preparing the big pot, which would take exactly twelve minutes to brew. This wasn't the first middle-of-the-night emergency on the Tremayne ranch, and that big pot had been used for every one of them.

Dusty finger-combed her sleep-tangled hair. "The wind sounds terrible," Nancy remarked.

"It woke me at one," Dusty said.

"Yes, I heard it in the night, too. It's coming from the north."

"I expected it to be raining by now."

"Or snowing," Nancy said. The big coffeepot began gurgling. "I'll get the thermos bottles ready."

Dusty went to the window. The tree branches were leaping around like things demented. Old leaves, twigs and dirt skittered along the ground at an alarming speed. The tall poles supporting the yard lights were swaying and casting ghostly rays that barely penetrated the density of the moving debris.

Nancy came back from the pantry with the thermos bottles. "Luke said the loose cattle could be the bulls."

"It's possible."

"Some of them are mean, Dusty, particularly in a wind like this. You be careful out there."

"Believe me, I don't intend tangling with a bull." Not all of the bulls were mean-tempered, but there were a few that everyone avoided riling, even Luke, who was afraid of nothing.

The men began coming out of the bunkhouse. Nancy filled the thermos bottles with hot coffee and Dusty capped them. First dawn was breaking, a barely noticeable lighting of the eastern sky.

Dusty left her hat on the hook and pulled on a warm jacket with a hood, and gloves. Gathering the thermos bottles, she said "See ya later" to Nancy and pushed the back door open. The wind hit her hard, tearing at her hair and clothing. Ahead, she could see Luke and the men leading horses and packing saddles into two trailers.

Bucking the wind, Dusty made her way to the pickups, horse trailers and men. In minutes, everything was ready to go. Everyone scrambled into the trucks, and Dusty ended up between Wyatt and Lyle. Michael was riding with Luke and Russ, and Bud's absence indicated that he was away from the ranch.

Wyatt seemed exhilarated with the adventure and talked while he drove. Lyle, who never said much under any circumstances, made brief responses to Wyatt. Dusty rode in silence, involved with her own thoughts.

Michael had probably never even been near a bull. Most of the animals were calm as long as there weren't any cows in season within smelling distance. But even the calmest animal could become agitated by this kind of wind, and there were two or three that were naturally high-strung and ornery.

She wished that Michael had stayed behind. He wasn't experienced enough to cope with a blinding wind and bad-tempered bulls. She should have said something to Luke, suggested that Michael be kept out of this.

It took about fifteen minutes to reach the stretch of highway Deputy Joe Rawlins had indicated. Dusty had been hoping the cattle had come from another pasture and she would see steers strung out along the road. No such luck. Three of the bulls were standing with their hindquarters to the wind, right next to the highway.

Luke's pickup drove off the highway and through the fallen section of fence. While Wyatt pulled off the road and stopped, Dusty watched Luke's truck making a sweep of the pasture. She knew what he was doing, checking to see if any of the bulls had chosen not to wander.

His truck came back and stopped. Everyone got out. "There's two at the far end of the field," Luke shouted to be heard above the wind.

The ranch owned nine bulls. Five were accounted for, which meant that four would have to be tracked down. The sky was getting a little lighter, although it would be another hour before true dawn broke.

Luke and Dusty examined the downed fence. "I don't think the wind did this," Dusty said. "Looks to me like one of the bulls walked through it." It was always a possibility; the bulls were strong enough to go anywhere they might take the notion. Under normal conditions, the sturdy posts and barbed wire kept the animals from roaming, but this wind was not at all normal.

One of the bulls at the side of the road snorted and pawed the ground. Dusty looked at the huge, angry animal. "Use the horses, Luke. Don't try leading them back."

"Right. They're worked up and aggravated." Luke started away, shouting to the men, "Unload the horses!"

Dusty grabbed his sleeve. "Do you have to involve Michael?"

Luke looked at her queerly. "I don't have to do anything, Dusty. Do you want me to leave him out of it?"

She hesitated. "He wouldn't like it, would he?"

"Being singled out and protected? Would you like it?"

Realizing that she couldn't do that to Michael, Dusty shook her head. "No, I wouldn't like it. Forget I said anything."

Luke nodded. "Don't worry. He's got a good head on his shoulders. He's not gonna do anything foolish."

"Not intentionally," Dusty whispered as Luke walked off, fighting the wind with every step.

There were four horses, and the four hired men, Lyle, Jack, Michael and Wyatt quickly saddled them and got to work. Luke stood near the opening in the fence, and Dusty went to stand by Wyatt's pickup. If there had been a fifth horse, she would have mounted and helped, but Luke was directing the show and seemed satisfied with its progress.

This was really the first time Dusty had watched Michael on horseback. He had a steady hand with the reins and seemed well in control. But it was still quite dark, and the air was turbulent with flying dust and debris. The horses were nervous in the wind, and the bulls didn't look at all cooperative.

Dusty didn't like the situation at all. Worriedly her gaze went farther out. Four of the bulls had wandered, and who knew how long the fence had been down? The animals could be miles away. They might have merely followed the highway, in which case they'd be easily found. But they could have gone into the mountains, which were barely visible in this light and turmoil. They were there, though, rugged and rocky and heavily treed, with a thousand hiding spots for stubborn animals.

The wind was cold. Dusty yanked up the hood of her jacket. The men had pulled their hats down low on their heads, but Dusty thought it was a miracle that they weren't blowing off and disappearing in the melee.

The four mounted men began urging the three bulls toward the hole in the fence. Dusty could hear snatches of whistles and voices. She kept her eyes on Michael, and caught her breath when a big red bull turned and charged at the riders. The horses pranced out of his way, and the bull stopped.

One of the bulls started walking in the right direction; the other two looked firmly planted. Dusty sighed nervously. The wind was the problem; the animals didn't want to face into it.

Finally, an eternity it seemed to Dusty, the three bulls were back in their pasture. Luke brought up the fallen barbed wire, and the other men dismounted to help secure the fence.

"They might not stay put," Jack warned while hammering a heavy-duty staple into a post.

"I have a feeling it was Rhino who knocked the fence down," Luke said. "He's always been spooky in high wind."

Rhino was one of the missing bulls, a big, black brute that Dusty had always been wary of. While the men finished repairing the fence, she got out the thermos jugs. Hot coffee was waiting for them on the lee side of one of the horse trailers.

They sipped coffee and speculated about the missing bulls, but it was ultimately decided that Jack and Wyatt should each take a pickup and scour the highway in both directions. Michael, Lyle, Luke and Dusty would search on horseback. The animals were valuable, each one worth upward of ten thousand dollars. Rhino, an Angus bull, would bring twenty-five thousand in a heartbeat.

Daylight was discouraging. The sky was heavy with dark storm clouds. Draining their coffee cups, everyone set out on their appointed jobs.

Dusty mounted the roan gelding that Wyatt had been riding. Each rider was to go in a different direction. The two pickups drove off, one going east, one going west. Dusty glanced at Michael and saw elation on his face. The damned man was enjoying this! She rode off with a disgruntled expression.

A couple of hours later, three of the four roving bulls had been secured in the pasture. Rhino was still missing.

So were Lyle and Michael.

Luke and Dusty discussed the situation. "They headed for the mountains," Luke said. "One of them probably picked up Rhino's trail."

"Maybe they're together," Dusty said hopefully. The thought of Michael by himself, meeting up with Rhino, gave her a chill. She'd seen adventure in his eyes, despite the miserable weather. Lyle knew what to do with Rhino, but she didn't trust Michael in his present daring mood. He might even think he should challenge the huge Angus, which could be a dire mistake.

Luke had other concerns on his mind. "Dusty, we've got to go back and check the hay tarps."

Every rick of hay on the ranch was covered with a heavy tarpaulin. This wind could destroy the ranch's hay supply. Dusty's anxious gaze swept the mountain vista. "What about Michael and Lyle?"

They were yelling to be heard. "They'll bring in Rhino, don't worry."

"I'm not worried about Rhino!"

"What d'ya want us to do? That hay is loose under the tarps. If the ropes give out, we'll lose a lot of feed."

Dusty needed reassurance. "But do you think Michael and Lyle will be all right?"

"Yeah, I do. It's up to you, though. If you want us to ride out and bring them back, that's what we'll do."

If it was any of the hands out there other than Michael, Dusty knew she wouldn't be forcing Luke to stand in the wind and debate the matter. Saving the hay was crucial, which she knew as well as Luke.

"We'll go back," she shouted.

Luke didn't waste any time. "Load up!" he yelled to the men.

Dusty got in Luke's pickup for the ride back, and Jack rode with Wyatt. Out of the wind and under way, she lowered her hood and uneasily smoothed down her hair. A burst of hindsight made her angry: Why hadn't she insisted that Michael drive one of the trucks and check the highway? Instead she'd let him go riding off on a damned horse!

By Luke's terse comments, she knew that he was engrossed in the problems caused by high wind. The other animals would be spooked, too. There were very young calves to consider. The hay and anything else not tied down could be blown clear into the next county.

Dusty tried to muster a concern to match Luke's, but she couldn't seem to think beyond Michael on horseback in unfamiliar country in a beast of a wind storm. Lyle would manage. As young as he was, Lyle knew what he was doing; Michael did not.

She was suddenly perspiring. "Luke..."

"Yeah?" He glanced from the road, and at that very moment something huge and heavy hit the windshield. "It's a tarp!" Luke yelled. The pickup swerved and the tarp fell away. "Damn!" Luke cried. "That was one of our hay tarps!"

Luke slammed on the brakes, jumped out of the pickup and ran back to retrieve the tarp.

With a hard, fast heartbeat, Dusty sat back. Every man was needed to secure the ricks of hay. Michael would be all right, she told herself. He would! She couldn't let herself think otherwise.

But she couldn't get "otherwise" out of her mind and sat stiffly and uncomfortably during the short ride. When they arrived at the compound, Luke and the men hurried to unhitch the horse trailers. They got back into the pickups and took off again, heading, Dusty knew, for the ricks, which were located in various fields.

Weary, discouraged and worried, Dusty battled the wind to the house and went in. Nancy was waiting. "I've got the radio on. Dusty, the wind has reached near-cyclone velocity. There are warnings out. We're in for a hard rainfall, too."

Dusty closed her eyes and groaned. "Michael and Lyle are out looking for Rhino. We got the other bulls back in their pasture, but Rhino's still missing."

Nancy went to the window. "And Luke?"

"He and the others are checking the hay. One of the tarps was flying around and hit the pickup." It struck Dusty that Nancy was as worried about her husband as she was about Michael, and her voice gentled. "Luke's fine, Nancy."

Nancy turned. "But you don't know about Michael. You're in love with him, aren't you?"

Dusty became very still. "Am I?"

"Don't you know?"

"I've been trying to...sort it out."

Nancy hesitated, then took Dusty's arm. "Come and sit down. I'll get you a cup of coffee and make some break-fast."

"I left the thermos bottles in the pickup," Dusty said dully as she sat at the kitchen table.

"Luke will bring them in later."

Dusty slowly slipped out of her jacket, letting it fall against the back of her chair. "Nancy...Michael and I...were married once."

Nancy turned from the counter with widened eyes. "You were what?"

"We were seventeen. Michael was spending the summer with family friends, the Linkmans. They owned what is now the Drucker place. We...eloped. Mom and Dad and the Linkmans found us shortly after the ceremony. Michael was sent back to New York on the first plane east and I never saw him again. Until Florida."

Nancy looked shell-shocked. She gave up on cooking and sat at the table. "I don't know what to say."

"Sounds like a soap opera, doesn't it?"

"It sounds...terribly sad. Dusty, I had no idea."

"How could you?" Dusty drew in a long, emotional breath. "Very few people know about it. It's not some-thing I talk about. To be honest, I rarely thought about it." She added, after a pause, "Anymore."

"Meeting him again must have knocked you for a loop."

Dusty sighed. "I couldn't believe it. He couldn't, ei-ther."

"He must still care for you. Maybe he never stopped caring. That's why he came to Wyoming and is trying to be a cowboy, to be near you."

Dusty shook her head. "Not entirely." She related the things Michael had said about wanting something different than what he'd had in New York.

"He could have found something different in a million places, Dusty. He's here because of you."

"If he cares so much for me," Dusty said with a spark of spirit, "why did he leave the way he did? Nancy, I understand how devastating unexpected tragedy can be. I went through it twice with Mom and Dad. It practically numbs a person, but..."

"But he could have found some way to let you know."

Dusty looked miserable. "Is my attitude horribly selfish? Nancy, it happened the very morning after...after a wonderful night together. Michael was supposed to join me for breakfast, and there was nothing from him, not a hint. What makes it seem so callous is that the lady he was staying with, a family friend, found the time to write a note to her gardener before she left on the same plane. Her gardener, Nancy! Wasn't I at least as important to Michael as Cora Potter's gardener was to her?"

Dusty was near tears. "What was I supposed to think? I was terribly hurt, positive that I wanted no more to do with Michael Crowley. A few days after I got home from Florida and you and Luke had left on your trip, Michael called. It stunned me that he would have the gall, and I cut him off short.

"Then, out of the blue, he showed up. He mentioned his father's death right away, but I didn't put it together with what happened in Florida. The next day, when he came back, he told me about the emergency call from his brother. He had to go, of course he had to go. I understand that. But couldn't he have left me something? Anything? Dammit, a note in the sand at the foot of my terrace stairs! Anything!"

Dusty put her elbow on the table and held her head. "Maybe if I hadn't had so many lousy experiences with men, Michael's sin wouldn't seem so enormous. I really can't deal with another failure."

Nancy was empathizing with Dusty's every word, but there was still fairness on her face. "You haven't discussed it with Michael, have you? Like this? Laying out your feelings, letting him know how badly you were hurt?"

"No." Dusty's hand dropped. "I'm angry with him, Nancy. Angry that he left the way he did in Florida, angry that he came here and asked for a job. His working as a cowhand is outrageous. The man is highly educated. He can't possibly need the piddling wages he's being paid."

"That's beside the point, Dusty. Don't equate it with money. Maybe he's getting something out of this job that he never received before."

"If he runs into Rhino he'll get something, all right." Agitated, Dusty got up and went to the window. "I'm worried sick about him." She frowned at the scene outside. "Nancy, the wind has stopped."

"It has?" Rising hurriedly, Nancy peered around Dusty to see through the window. "My Lord, look at that sky."

Black and strangely yellow, the sky looked ready to fall in. Everything was still. No trees moved, no dust flew. "I've never seen anything like it," Dusty said in a near whisper. "What's happening?"

"I don't know, but when it starts again, it's going to be a doozy. I wish Luke and the men would come inside."

"Michael...and Lyle," Dusty whispered. She whirled and nearly knocked Nancy down in the process. "I'm sorry." Dusty ran and grabbed her jacket. "When Luke gets back, tell him that I've gone looking for Michael and Lyle."

"Dusty, you can't go out in this! Anything could happen!"

"Tell Luke not to worry and not to come looking for me. I know every inch of this ranch, better than he does. I thought Lyle had more sense than to stay out in this kind of weather, but maybe he doesn't." Dusty zipped her jacket.

"And I'm beginning to think that Michael has no sense at all. Neither one of them are going to get hurt, not if I can help it. See ya, Nancy."

Nancy followed her friend to the door. "Dusty, be careful!"

Dusty was already running toward the barn. She turned and skipped backward. "I do love him, Nancy—the big jerk! And when I find him, I'm liable to smack him one!" She saw Nancy shake her head, a helpless expression on her face. "And don't worry! I'll be fine!"

Ten

On horseback Dusty cut cross-country, aiming for Michael's initial direction from the bulls' pasture. Lyle was on her mind, unquestionably, but Michael was her primary target. It was absurd that he was out here in the weirdest storm setting she'd ever seen. Right now the area seemed to be in the eye of a storm with cyclone intensity. Nancy was probably right: When it started again, it could be a doozy.

Dusty loosened her jacket. With the atmosphere so still and sluggish, the temperature was almost warm. Humid, too. She glanced up at the ominous yellowish sky and black clouds that looked ready to burst, and urged her horse into a faster pace. A series of lightning flashes startled her, the first she'd seen.

Within an hour she'd picked up Michael's trail. There was evidence of recent shoe marks in spots of sandy ground, at any rate, which indicated the passage of a horse. What bothered Dusty was a second set of tracks, made by unshod hooves.

But if Michael was on Rhino's trail, what was keeping Lyle busy? The youth was too experienced to dawdle with a cold trail.

Dusty looked behind her. Maybe Lyle had already headed for home. She was riding in the hills and they could easily have missed seeing each other.

Besides, she told herself, Lyle could take care of himself and Michael couldn't, especially if that second set of tracks was Rhino's.

Dusty had been taught the fine art of tracking by her father. Long before she ever met Michael Crowley, she had accompanied Walt Tremayne and his friends on hunting trips into the mountains. She'd been avidly interested in the variety of trails left by deer, bear, moose and elk. Cattle and horse tracks were so common, she'd needed no instruction.

It was handy knowledge to have at a time like this and brought back memories of her father and their hunting excursions. But Dusty dwelled on the more carefree days of her youth for only a short while. The gathering storm, so unusual to her eyes, was unnerving. Lightning was streaking through the eerie clouds, with rolling, rumbling thunder coming behind it. The best possible scenario would be in catching up with Michael and getting him back to the ranch before all hell broke loose. The worst would be getting caught in the open in a lethal electrical storm.

Dusty grimaced; Michael was probably green enough to seek shelter under a tree.

She shook her head. Even a greenhorn knew better than that!

Her faith in Michael's abilities was depressingly skimpy. The man was far from stupid, so why was she so afraid for his safety?

Dusty topped a sizable hill and stopped her horse to look over the immense valley below. It rose on the other side in a long, gradual slope that culminated in another hill, much like her present vantage point. She'd always thought this area looked as though a giant scoop had taken a smooth, massive bite out of the earth. The ground cover was sketchy at this time of year, mostly sage and dried clumps of last season's bunchgrass. Today it looked particularly barren, as dark and forbidding as the black clouds over her head.

But coming down the opposite slope, appearing as no more than the most miniature of silhouettes, was a horse and rider. Elation filled her. It was Michael, she was positive.

A tremendous bolt of lightning split the sky, followed almost immediately by a cracking, explosive clap of thunder. In the next instant, rain began falling.

"Oh, damn," she whispered, and kicked her horse in the ribs. The animal leaped forward and was running like a wild thing in seconds. Dusty leaned forward and rode like she'd never ridden before. Outrunning the storm was impossible; it was upon her in all of its fury. The wind was gaining force, the rain was a deluge; she was soaked through in minutes, but she kept the horse at a hard run.

It was a long way to the low point in the valley, and she lost sight of Michael in the rain. But she kept going and finally saw him again, riding hard, too, coming right at her.

She never slowed down, but streaked past Michael yelling, "Follow me!" A glance back showed Michael turning his horse and running him again, keeping up, riding low on the animal's back, as she was. She could hear the two horses' labored breathing, even with thunder and lightning crashing in her ears.

"Where...going?" was all she caught of Michael's shout.

"To a line shack," she yelled. "Keep going!"

Over her shoulder she got a glimpse of his face below his soggy hat brim and saw grim determination, exactly the emotion she was feeling. A burst of exhilaration sped through her. They would make it, the line shack was only another few miles.

The hard beating of the horses' hooves became a steady rhythm. There were hills that slowed them down on one side and gave them increased speed on the other. Dusty spotted a grove of dark spindly trees through the rain and breathed more freely, the line shack was nestled within the lodgepole pines.

She pulled her horse up in the clearing around the cabin and dismounted before the animal was completely stopped. The storm was deafening, forcing her to shout. "There's a corral out back. Unsaddle. We'll put the horses in the corral and bring the saddles inside."

They moved quickly. The storm was gaining momentum, the wind and rain becoming fierce. Bucking the elements, they dropped the saddles onto the ground and led the heaving horses to the corral.

"Come on, let's get inside!" Dusty ran and Michael followed. They picked up the saddles and made for the cabin.

The small one-room shack felt like sanctuary once the door was closed behind them. Water streamed from their clothing. Dusty shook the wet hair out of her eyes and dropped her saddle in a corner.

Michael stood and looked at her. "What in hell's name are you doing out here?"

Taken aback, Dusty turned. "Looking for you and Lyle, what else? Put your saddle next to mine. We'll wipe them down later." She saw Michael's expression as disapproving. "You preferred remaining in the open in this kind of storm? Did you know this place was here?"

"No, I didn't know it was here," Michael said sharply. "But that's not reason enough for you to risk your life!"

A bout of shivers hit Dusty. "Tell me you're not as ungrateful as you sound," she stammered through quivering lips.

Michael dropped his saddle. "You're cold. Dammit, you're wet clear through!"

"So are you! Worry about yourself, okay?"

Michael threw up his hands. "I'm grateful! Is that what you want to hear? I'm glad to be under a roof and out of the rain. Now, get out of those wet clothes." Striding to one of the two narrow beds in the room, Michael yanked off the top blanket and tossed it to her. "You can wear this until your clothes dry."

"Who pronounced you king of the hill?"

"Your teeth are chattering, *boss*, which sort of weakens that tough-guy image you try so hard to project."

"I do no such thing! What's wrong with you? I rode clear out here to... to save your butt, and what thanks do I get? I should have let Rhino gore your arrogant hide!"

"Rhino! Is *he* why you came to my rescue?" Laughing shortly, Michael took off his soaked hat and slapped it against his thigh to dislodge some of its moisture.

His brief laugh annoyed Dusty. "I don't think Rhino's particularly funny."

"Rhino's a sweetheart. For your information, he's safe and sound in a box canyon about five miles from here."

Dusty formed a saccharine smile. "I suppose you put him there."

"As a matter of fact, I did." Michael's expression became deadly serious when Dusty sneezed. "Get out of those clothes or I'll do it for you."

She had to do it, but Michael issuing orders went against her grain. "I'll do it when I feel like doing it!"

"You'll do it now." Michael began advancing. "*Now*, Dusty."

She backed up. "Now who's projecting a tough-guy image?" She threw the blanket at him. "*You* undress! You're as wet as I am!"

Michael stopped. "I'll concede that point." He pulled off his denim jacket and started unbuttoning his shirt. "For now."

Dusty stared until she realized that he was really going to strip. Her stomach suddenly felt hollow. The storm was horrible. They were stuck in this line shack until God knew when, and they couldn't stay in their wet clothes without risking pneumonia. She wasn't merely damp, she was cold and saturated clear to the skin.

So was Michael.

She turned her back to him just as he reached for his belt buckle. Concentrating on something other than the man undressing behind her took effort, but there were other things to consider.

The shack had a stove, they could build a fire, *if* there was wood in the storage box. And if things were normal, there should be some canned goods and coffee in the cabin's one small cupboard. There was a hand-operated water pump inside, but one had to follow a path to the outhouse for more personal needs. All in all, they could wait out the storm in reasonable comfort.

Finding Michael had been her goal, and she shouldn't be feeling edgy about having succeeded. But he expected her to believe that he'd located Rhino and tucked the bull in a box canyon, all by himself?

She cleared her throat. "Have you seen anything of Lyle?"

"Our paths crossed a while back. He said he was heading for a place called Rocky Gorge."

"Rocky Gorge!"

"That's what he said. Why? Something wrong with Rocky Gorge?"

"Well, you were obviously following Rhino's tracks. Didn't Lyle see them?"

"No, I picked up the trail after we separated again. I'm covered now, you can turn around."

Complying, Dusty couldn't hold back a laugh. "You look funny in that blanket."

"So will you." Michael studied her for a moment. "Then again, maybe you in nothing but a blanket won't be at all funny. Are you waiting for me to help you out of those clothes?"

"I don't need any help, thank you very much!"

"Fine, but get to it." Michael walked over to the stove. "Does this work?"

"Yes, if there's any wood in the box. Check it, and keep your back turned."

Getting out of soggy clothes wasn't a simple matter. Her jacket went quickly, but her jeans and shirt were sticking to her skin. Shivering, Dusty began peeling the garments away from her goose bumps. Naked and shaking, she snagged another blanket from a bed and wrapped it around herself. It was prickly but dry, although she wondered if she would ever feel really warm again.

"There's wood," Michael announced from the storage box.

Looking around the cabin, Dusty spotted a coil of heavy rope. After locating a butcher knife she cut a section from the coil and tied it around herself and the blanket. "Do you want a belt? I'm decent, you can look now."

Michael did so. "Just as I thought. I don't feel a bit like laughing."

Her cheeks, at least, were warm, Dusty acknowledged, and why she should be blushing over Michael's comment when she'd told Nancy right out that she was in love with him was a mystery.

Maybe it was because he seemed so different. Had he really driven Rhino into a box canyon? Hadn't he been worried about the storm? What had she visualized from him once she'd found him, intense relief that she'd rushed to his rescue?

She was getting very strange vibes from Michael, which she'd just as soon put off thinking about for now. Becoming very efficient, Dusty moved to the stove and opened its small front door. "Bring some wood. I'll build a fire."

"How about me building the fire?"

Her gaze collided with his. "Do you know how?"

He smirked. "Yes, Dusty, I know how to build a fire."

Her face colored again. "Well, how would I know what you know?"

"What makes you think I'm so damned helpless?"

"You actually resent my coming out here to look for you!"

"What I resent is your taking an unnecessary chance!" Michael retorted. "Do you think I haven't seen this kind of storm before?"

Feeling foolish all of a sudden, Dusty walked away. Of course he'd seen storms before. The East Coast endured as many storms as Wyoming did.

She pumped water and prepared the coffeepot while Michael built a very good fire. While she worked, she eyed the piles of wet clothing. Setting the coffeepot on the top of the stove, she got the coil of rope and began looking for a place to string it.

"What're you doing?" Michael questioned.

"If we don't hang those wet things, they'll never dry."

"Will that rope stretch from wall to wall?"

"It's longer than that." Dusty hefted the rope, which was thick and sturdy and much longer than she needed for a clothesline.

"Then give it to me."

Dusty handed him the rope and watched while he strung it from a hook on a window frame to a nail on the opposite wall, leaving the excess length of it coiled on the floor. "Will that do?"

"It'll do nicely, thanks."

"Go sit by the stove and warm up. I'll hang your clothes."

"Michael . . ." Her voice sounded impatient. He gave her a look that squelched further protest, but she didn't sit down and she didn't go near the stove. After a few moments of watching him drape wet clothes over the rope, she turned her back and went to a window.

It was raining too hard to see out, but she stood there and stared at the water running down the windowpanes. The cabin was beginning to lose its chill; it wouldn't be long before it was warm and toasty inside. But her uneasiness surpassed physical discomfort and even the raging storm outside.

"What is this place?" Michael asked.

"A line shack. There are several on the ranch. The men stay in them during roundup. They're sometimes used in hunting season, too."

"Do you summer your cattle this far out?"

"Farther than this." She felt Michael come up behind her, and gathered the blanket a little closer around herself, shivering again, but doing so more from internal pressures than from the temperature.

"Are you getting warm?"

"Yes, thanks." Dusty felt him at her back, although he hadn't touched her. Her stomach seemed knotted, and not because of the storm. "Our relationship has been...far from normal, hasn't it?"

"I'd say so." Very gently, Michael began separating the strands of her wet hair. He felt her stiffen. "Relax. This isn't a pass."

It felt good, his fingers in her hair, and she closed her eyes. Sensation riffled through her, light, dancing waves of pleasure that reminded and teased and gave courage to her tongue. "You've...intruded on my life," she whispered.

"I suppose I have."

"To what goal?" Dusty turned suddenly. "Tell me, Michael. The truth. Why did you come to Wyoming?"

His gaze washed over her face. "What do you want to hear? That I came because of you?"

"I don't want to hear anything but the truth."

"Do you think I would have come if you weren't here?"

"It's possible. After what you said about being discontent in New York, anything's possible."

"Not too plausible, though. If we hadn't met again in Florida, I probably wouldn't have even thought of Wyoming."

"But you can't say it right out, can you? You can't say, 'Dusty, I'm here because of you.' Why not, Michael?"

He was silent, thoughtful. "Maybe because I'm leery of your reaction."

She gave a sharp laugh. "What do you think I'd do, turn on you?"

"I'm not sure. You don't trust me, Dusty." He peered down at her. "Do you?"

Uncomfortable with his change of emphasis, she walked away. Behind her she heard, "You just answered my question."

She whirled. "Oh no you don't! You're not going to put words in my mouth!"

"Then you do trust me?"

Her chin came up. "I didn't say that, either." She had, after all, ample reason for mistrust. Or, more accurately, ample reason for a *lack* of trust.

He looked so silly in that blanket, and whatever innuendo he'd intended with his remarks about not laughing over how she looked, she felt silly. How could two people conduct a serious conversation under these circumstances?

Besides, he was being evasive. This probably was not the best time to dig into each other's psyche and motivations.

Dusty glanced around the room, then back to Michael with a jolting awareness. He might look silly, but he was naked under that blanket. His hair was tousled and damp, his eyes glowing. He might not be in the mood for behavioral analysis, but he was in a mood. They were alone and isolated, and she'd seen that same expression on his face in Florida.

The air was suddenly seething with moods, hers as well as his. She could stop it from accelerating, by words, by actions. She knew how to extinguish sexual tension in a man, she'd done it many times.

Only, she loved this foolish, stubborn man—this man who'd labored over books for years to attain a law degree, then decided he wanted something else—and her own emotions were *not* extinguishable. Not any longer.

He *was* here because of her, even if he was reluctant to say so in precise phrases, and she did love him, despite doubts about his abilities and even uneasy questions about his good sense.

Wind and rain battered the cabin, adding to the emotional turbulence within. Dusty wasn't even slightly chilled anymore. She was not averse to making the first move.

Rather, the thought of letting him know what she wanted was exhilarating.

His eyes were on her, and she saw a dare in their dark blue depths. Neither of them was thinking of conversation . . . or controversy. The mounting tension created spiky thrills in Dusty's system.

She deliberately dislodged a flap of the blanket, baring a shoulder, and saw a narrowing of his eyes, a tightening of muscle and skin. He took one small step forward and spoke in a hoarse, gravelly voice. "If we play, it's for keeps this time, Dusty."

Her spirit soared but she arched an eyebrow. "Whatever are you intimating, Michael?"

"The whole ball of wax. I want it all or . . . nothing."

Flirtatious and a little giddy now, she bared the other shoulder. "You mean you *won't* play without a commitment?"

"Don't tease."

But teasing was exactly what she wanted. She wanted to stretch his limits, to bring him to the point of utter honesty. Maybe she needed to hear him admit what a cad he'd been in Florida. Wouldn't that ease the ache haunting her? A simple admission: *Dusty, I totally and completely forgot you. I'm sorry, more sorry than I can say, but that's what happened.*

She smiled, a slow, sensual curving of lips that rocketed through Michael with the impact of an electrical shock. She was certain, he realized, that she was the stronger-willed. She wanted, at this moment, to bring him to his knees. Whether she knew it or not, this was the moment of truth for them, brought about, perhaps, by a subconscious need of hers to exact revenge for her interpretation of what had occurred in Florida.

He could deal with it. Dusty deserved the tables turned on her more than any person he'd ever known. He loved her madly, but his feelings were not tools to be used against him. She didn't like him working as a cowhand, which was just plain tough. He was who he was, and happy for the first time in years. She was not going to destroy that for him, nor was she going to lead him around by the nose.

He untied the rope at his waist and saw surprise on her face. "You want to play? We'll play."

"But..." Her eyes widened as his blanket fell to the floor. Stark naked, he walked toward her. Her gaze flicked downward, then up quickly. He was fully aroused.

Courage and bravado deserted her in one massive swoop. "Michael... I..."

He pulled her forward and the top of her blanket also deserted her. In the next heartbeat her bare breasts were against his chest. He held the back of her head and looked into her eyes. "You're like the storm, Dusty, wild and exciting. No man could say no to you."

"But..." His mouth on hers eliminated further speech. Quite suddenly, she didn't care. Her eyes closed as a low moan built in her throat. His lips caressed hers, tasted hers. His tongue probed and tantalized. His hand kneaded her scalp, while his other untied the rope around her blanket. In seconds there was no barrier or cloth between them, only hot female skin against hot male skin.

Her feelings were escaping from the tight rein she'd been attempting since Michael's shocking appearance at the ranch. He was not passively submitting to seduction, he was the seducer, and there wasn't a passive cell in his extremely aroused body.

Lightning and thunder and beating rain went unnoticed, trivial compared to the raging desire inside the cabin. Michael scooped her up off her feet and carried her to one of the single beds. The line shack was not meant for leisure and not equipped for lovers.

But even the floor would have done for Dusty. On her back on the narrow bed, she welcomed Michael's weight and was thrilled by his harsh breathing, the feverish heat of his body, the intensity of his kisses.

Neither was thinking of game-playing now, nor of which was the stronger-willed. Nothing mattered but their need for each other. They writhed and moved and kissed and touched, and the need grew until it was unbearable.

Dusty was weeping. Not intentionally, but tears were seeping from her eyes and she couldn't halt them. "Michael . . . oh, Michael." Her voice was barely recognizable, rasping and rusty.

"Dusty, baby," he whispered thickly. The small bed was restricting. They either had to remain stacked or snuggled on their sides. He stayed where he was, leading Dusty deeper and deeper into passion, taking her farther and farther away from past hurts and any thoughts of vengeance.

Her legs opened, making space for his hips. Kisses became brief and gasping. Hands searched, managing to arouse further, even in their tight quarters.

Dazed, teary-eyed and nearly mindless with need, Dusty moved enough to align their bodies. "Do it . . . make love to me."

Michael raised his head and spoke raggedly. "I have nothing with me. It doesn't matter to me, but you should know."

"It . . . doesn't matter to me, either."

"Are you sure?"

She looked directly into his eyes. "You wanted the whole ball of wax. Maybe you'll get it."

Contention was present again, the events in Florida shining in two sets of eyes. Michael dampened his lips. "I meant what I said." He kissed the corner of her mouth. "I hope to prove to you someday that what happened in Florida wasn't what you thought."

Dusty closed her eyes. Her body was racked with desire. She didn't want to talk about Florida, she didn't even want to think about it. With all of his many faults and flaws, she loved the man upon her. She loved his nudity and the solidity of his body, his hair, his face, his hands. Easily, very easily, she could tell him so.

But hints, even blatant ones, were not the same as confessions of love, and she'd heard nothing about love from Michael.

"Don't talk," she whispered. "Not now."

Michael hadn't so much as looked at another woman since Florida, and for a long time before that. Talking wasn't what he wanted now, either. Burrowing his hands beneath her hips, he lifted her and slid into the velvety heat of her body.

Dusty's breath caught. "Look at me," Michael commanded. Her eyes fluttered open, and the emotion in his stunned her. She raised her hands to his face, one on each cheek and whispered. "What have we done to each other?"

His lips sought hers and she felt a tremendous shudder in his body.

And then there was no more speaking, there were no more questions. Possession of each other was all-consuming. They moved together on the narrow bed, advancing and retreating in complete harmony. Inarticulate sounds of hunger accompanied the dance of love, quick, needful kisses, soft moans of pleasure.

Time seemed to stand still. Dusty ran her hands down Michael's sweat-slicked back to his tight, firm buttocks. They rose, she rose, they fell, she yielded. The swirling pools of ecstasy gathered and intensified within her. She was being swiftly brought to the peak, and she reached for that ultimate pleasure with every cell in her body.

She began to cry out with each breath, a low, keening sound that fed her own passion, and Michael's. She clasped her lover to her, tightly, holding him as though she would never let go.

The intensity of her release rocked her, and she sobbed low and emotionally into the crook of Michael's neck while he attained the same beautiful moment.

They lay as they were for a long time. Dusty listened to the rain and gently stroked Michael's back. Her body was sated, at peace, as she was certain his was.

But physical expression and satisfaction, as important as they were, were only portions of a relationship.

"You meant what you said?" she asked quietly.

Michael lifted his head. "I meant it." They looked into each other's eyes.

Do you love me?

You don't trust me.

Wasn't he going to say more? Should she guess at his meaning? She wasn't opposed to being the first to say the word "marriage," but should she also be the first to mention "love."

Dusty's gaze slid from his. "I'd better get up. We did take a chance."

Michael kept staring. "You said it didn't matter."

"I would rather let things...take a more natural course."

He shook her gently. "Will you go out with me now? Spend time with me on my free days?"

"Yes," she whispered faintly, hurt and trying to hide it. Why couldn't they speak openly and honestly? Now was the time to do so, if they were ever going to.

She hoped Michael didn't see the tears in her eyes while she slipped from the bed . . . and him.

Eleven

Dusty braved the storm—which, thank God, was beginning to slow down—for a trip to the outhouse. Her heart felt shattered and she wasn't sure why. She could have said "I love you" just as easily as Michael. Maybe he'd been waiting to hear how she felt. He had admitted, after all, that he was leery of her reactions.

When she returned to the cabin, her tears were no wetter than the rain on her face, which voided their import. She was startled, however, to see Michael dressed and pulling on his boots.

"Your clothes couldn't possibly be dry," she exclaimed.

"No, but they're just going to get wet again." Michael got up and pulled his denim jacket from the rope.

Dusty stared with big eyes. "Are you leaving? Michael, the storm isn't over!"

"Tell me something. If you'd been at Rocky Gorge when the storm broke, where would you have gone?"

"Gone? Well...this would be the closest...and most logical place," she said slowly with a dawning uneasiness.

"That's what I thought. I started wondering about it while you were outside. Dusty, it's obvious that Lyle's not here, but why isn't he?"

Suddenly weak-kneed, Dusty sank to the edge of the bed. "He...may have found other cover."

Michael dropped his jacket and kneeled in front of her. "Think hard. You know the area. Is there any other cover?"

Dusty thought of Rocky Gorge, which was dangerous on a sunny day, an abnormality of deep canyons, narrow crevices and needlelike spires. She could see why Lyle had deemed it necessary to check the gorge for Rhino. Cattle had wandered into it before and not all of them had been led back out safely.

"No," she said weakly, struck nearly dumb now by how remiss she'd been. She had thought of Lyle, but her concern had been focused on Michael. She clenched her hands into fists and brought them to her forehead. Lyle should be here. Something must have stopped him from riding in hard and fast, just as she and Michael had arrived. "My Lord."

Michael got to his feet. "I'm going out to look for him."

Dusty leaped up. "No, not in this! I'll go! You stay here. You don't even know where Rocky Gorge is located!"

Michael's eyes became narrowed and hard. "What the hell kind of person do you think I am? Do you actually believe I would stay here and let you go out there by yourself?" He pointed an angry finger. "*You* stay here! Just tell me where to go!"

Panic welled. "Michael, please listen to me. You have no idea what you might run into. Rocky Gorge is no place for a...a greenhorn."

He bent over and picked up his jacket. "You know something, Dusty? I don't find that word as insulting as you try to make it sound."

"I am not trying to insult you, but facts are facts!"

"Yes, they are. Fact number one, which you'd better get straight in your pretty head, honey. You're not going to tell me when to jump and how high." Michael came closer. "I care about you. I care a whole hell of a lot. But that doesn't make you my keeper.

"Fact number two. I'm going out to look for Lyle. I'd like you to stay here, but as stubborn and high-handed as you are, you'll probably traipse along in the rain." Michael went for his hat. "How do I find Rocky Gorge?"

Stung by his little speech, she was glad to reveal her upper hand. "I'm not going to tell you."

Michael gave her a deadly look. "If that's the way you want it, fine. I'll find it on my own." He started for the door.

"Michael!" Rushing forward, Dusty grabbed his arm. "Please . . ."

Their gazes tangled. "Please what, Dusty? Obey you? What if something happened to Lyle? He's little more than a boy, for God's sake!"

She could argue that Lyle knew a lot more about the rigors and dangers of ranch living than Michael did, but worry for the young man had her half sick. Just how would Michael, rushing headlong into something he had no experience with, help Lyle, though?

Michael was determined, adamant, she saw. Her chin came up. "I'm coming along. Wait while I get dressed."

"Dusty, just tell me where to go. There's no reason for you to get soaked again."

"I don't jump that easily, either, Michael."

A stare-down concluded in an exasperated sigh from Michael. "It never occurred to me that you might. I'll saddle the horses while you dress."

The wind had let up but the rain was a steady downpour, drenching sage, grass and anyone out in it. What had been dust was mud. Visibility was poor. The horses walked with their heads down.

Dusty was utterly miserable physically, plus she was sick-to-her-stomach worried about Lyle and resentful of Michael.

At the last minute he'd gone back into the cabin for the coil of rope, which she wished she had thought of first. Just when had he become so annoyingly efficient? Why would he think of taking along a rope, which was only sensible, when she'd been wallowing in anger and self-pity?

Dusty tossed her head. Maybe she *didn't* love him. Maybe she wanted no more to do with him. Maybe, after this lousy day was over, she'd send him packing. That would show him who was going to jump and when!

Michael kept his horse just a little behind Dusty's. She was stewing, he knew, madder than hell that he'd told her where the bear did it in the buckwheat. He grinned slightly at the analogy but his spurt of good humor didn't last for long.

This was not a carefree excursion, not by a long shot. He was bone-deep worried about Lyle. Rain was trickling into every possible opening of his clothing. He and Dusty should be wearing waterproof ponchos, which he knew full well the ranch possessed. The abrupt way the day had started had precluded much planning, however, and it had pretty much gone downhill from there.

Michael knew that Dusty was worried about Lyle, too, along with being ticked at him. Worse, though, she was blaming herself for whatever might have befallen the young cowhand. It was possible that Lyle was just fine, but Michael couldn't rely on "possibilities," not until he saw the boy with his own eyes. That might not happen until he and Dusty returned to ranch headquarters, but before they made that ride, he intended checking Lyle's last known destination. Thoroughly.

He genuinely wished that Dusty had stayed at the line shack. She could have given him the directions to Rocky Gorge; her being out in the incessant rain made little sense.

On the other hand, she could probably no more have stayed behind than he could.

They were suddenly, it seemed to Michael, riding among a veritable sea of gray and white boulders. The path narrowed. Dusty held the lead.

"How much farther?" Michael called.

"We're almost there."

Dusty was internally torn to shreds. She was scared for Lyle and relieved that Michael had thought of the young man. Simultaneously she was upset that she'd let Lyle's safety slide right past her, while being miffed at Michael on a personal level. All in all, she wasn't in the best of moods, and it was very easy to dwell on the Florida episode.

The time was fast approaching for a showdown. She had a few things to lay on Michael Crowley, a number of opinions and facts that she'd kept bottled up long enough.

Recognizing that the gorge was just ahead, Dusty stopped her horse and looked back at Michael. Enormous boulders paralleled the narrow trail, which restricted the horses' movements. "It gets a little tricky from here on," she announced coolly. "We'll be on a ledge with a deep drop-off on our right. There's plenty of room for the horses in single file, so keep a fairly loose rein and let the animal do the work."

Her expression was so cold and withdrawn, Michael inwardly cringed. At that moment he wanted to say, "Dusty, I love you. I know you see me as incompetent, but I'm not. Trust me, sweetheart."

Instead he said, "Let me take the lead."

She turned away. "No...I think not."

Michael shook his head and mumbled, "Stubborn damned female."

Dusty pretended she hadn't heard. Right now she wanted to concentrate on Lyle, and she hadn't exaggerated the danger of the trail ahead. The horses weren't afraid of heights and would follow the ledge as surefootedly as they walked on level ground. But a rider could tense up and cause all sorts of problems, which was why she'd warned Michael to relax and let his horse do the work.

Clicking her tongue, Dusty urged her horse away from the boulders and onto the ledge. The gorge was so misty with rain, she could hardly see across it. This was not where she expected to find Lyle, but she began calling his name, just in case. "Lyle! Are you here? Lyle!"

The ledge wound around a mountain of bare granite on a gradually descending plane. At the bottom of this first huge canyon, what was normally a dry wash was rushing with wild white water. Dusty could hear its speed and fury. For the most part, the area had needed a good drenching so she couldn't resent a hard rainfall. But she'd never seen the gorge quite like this.

Her voice fell flatly against the rain, when ordinarily voices echoed in the gorge. Wanting to see over the ledge, Dusty dismounted at a wide spot. Michael got down, too, and walked over to her. "Did you see or hear something?"

"No." Kneeling, Dusty peered down into the chasm. Her heart lurched at the unobstructed view of crashing water. If something—or someone—should fall in, it would be their end.

"Lyle wouldn't have stayed on this ledge, once the storm broke," she said in a strange, unsteady voice. Rocky Gorge was frightening today, and if Lyle was here...

He wouldn't be here if he could help it. Dusty's system recoiled at the horrifying thought.

Hearing movement behind her, she looked for its source and saw that Michael had led his horse around hers! She jumped to her feet. "That was a damned dumb thing to do just to prove a point! This ledge isn't wide enough for two horses!"

"Apparently it is," Michael said dryly. Putting his foot in the stirrup, he swung up onto the saddle. "Ready?"

Seething, with her eyes shooting daggers, she mounted. Just wait, she thought furiously. Just wait until Lyle's safe and this is over. You are really going to get it, buster, with both barrels!

Michael nudged his horse forward. He wasn't thinking of Dusty's anger, which was as obvious as the rain, because he was completely wrapped up in the missing cowhand. Instinct told him that Lyle was here, somewhere in this eerie, misty, noisy gorge. Possibly injured.

The feeling was so strong Michael trusted it implicitly. While Dusty called Lyle's name, he listened, closely, carefully.

Rounding a sharp curve on the ledge, Michael stopped his horse. Dusty couldn't see what he could, and he turned to look at her. "Lyle's horse is up ahead, just standing there."

Dusty's heart nearly stopped. "Michael..." She caught her breath. "Hurry...oh, hurry!"

It wasn't far to the drenched, forlorn-looking animal, and this time when Dusty dismounted, she was terrified of what she might see when she peered over the ledge. To her intense relief, Lyle was in plain sight. But he was yards below Dusty's level and on his back, lying on another ledge, a narrow outcropping of rock that was mere inches above the waterline. "Lyle! Can you hear me?"

Lyle lifted his head. "Dusty? Is that you?"

"It's me, Lyle. We were looking for you."

Michael was on his knees. "Lyle...are you injured?"

"Mac? You here, too? Hey, it's good to hear voices. I think I broke my leg."

"What happened?"

"Lightning struck only a few feet ahead of my horse. Scared 'im into rearing. Lost my seat. Mac, I'm sure glad to see ya."

Mac...Michael. Dusty's head reeled, but did it really matter what the men called him? A nickname was an honor, actually, denoting acceptance.

Lyle was glad she was here, Dusty realized, but it was Michael who gave him confidence. She eyed the rushing water swirling around Lyle's small space. "We've got to get him off that ledge," she said quietly.

"And quickly," Michael added. "That water's going to keep rising as long as it's raining. Lyle? I've got an idea. Stay put and don't worry. We'll have you out of there in no time."

"All right, Mac," Lyle yelled.

"What's your idea?" Dusty questioned as she followed Michael to his horse. He took the coil of rope from the saddle horn.

"To go down and get him," Michael stated flatly. "It's the only way. He can't climb up a rope with a broken leg."

Dusty's stomach fell clear to her knees. "There must be another way. Let's think about it."

"There's little time to waste."

"Michael, I know it's got to be done, but..." Dusty drew a breath and tried to calm herself. She knew she had to be pale, she *felt* pale. They had to rescue Lyle at whatever cost to themselves. If she was there alone, she wouldn't hesitate to go down that rope and do everything she could to get him away from that angry water.

But the thought of Michael doing it made her ill.

"I don't suppose you'd let me do it," she said hoarsely.

"Don't even think it!"

Dusty's anger flared. "There are times when I don't like you very much!"

Michael cocked an eyebrow, stared at her hard, then reached out with his free hand and clamped it around the back of Dusty's neck. His mouth came down on hers. Startled, Dusty tugged at his arm and growled angry, wordless invectives.

But then the force of her own feelings for this arrogant, unusual man exploded, and she began kissing him back. They clung together for a few moments, until Michael raised his head and looked into her eyes. "I'd like to take you right this second. In the rain, in the mud, it wouldn't matter," he whispered thickly. "Later, sweetheart, and don't try to convince me again that you don't like me."

Her lips were stinging and so were her eyes. "What...can I do to help?"

"You can help anchor the rope."

They worked with haste, in tune as they'd never been before. Dusty refused to think about selfishness, because it wasn't herself she'd been worried about. It still wasn't.

She'd go over that ledge in a heartbeat to help Lyle, to help anyone.

She just couldn't bear the thought of Michael doing it.

When he disappeared over the lip of the ledge, she leaned out to watch him with her breath held. If he slipped...if he fell into that raging torrent...

Her heart was pounding in her ears and every emotion, every drop of life in her body seemed to come together and teeter on the edge of a startling reality: She didn't care what he did today, or had done yesterday or would do tomorrow. She loved him.

It didn't matter that he'd forgotten her in Florida, it didn't matter that he'd exchanged a proud, lucrative career in law for boots and jeans on a cattle ranch. She'd loved him at seventeen, she'd loved him again in Florida and she loved him now.

"Be careful," she whispered. "Please be careful."

Michael was rappeling down the sheer face of the cliff. He'd anchored the rope in a way that was strange to Dusty, so that there appeared to be two ropes; one was wrapped around his waist, the other one was taut and used to support his descent.

Watching intently, missing none of his agility, she realized that he knew what he was doing. For that matter, he knew a lot more about dancing down the side of a rock bluff than she did.

Michael's feet landed on the small ledge. Lyle shaped the hint of a grin. "Good to see ya, Mac."

"Glad to see you're in one piece, Lyle." Michael got down on his knees. The boy's twisted leg was proof of a serious break. "Is your leg your only injury?"

"Think so. Got the wind knocked out of me, but that passed."

"Good. Lyle, you're going to have to hang on to my back for the climb up. Can you do it?"

"Yeah, Mac, I can do it."

"Let's get started then. I'm going to tie one end of this rope around your waist. We'll get you sitting up, then I'll turn around. Wrap your arms around my neck and hang on. If you feel yourself slipping or feeling faint, let me know.''

When Dusty realized that Michael was going to attempt to carry Lyle on his back, she started crying. She would say nothing, this had to be done. But Lyle was a strapping young man, and how, in God's name, would Michael find the strength to climb the cliff with so much weight on his back?

She had never witnessed such an act of utter courage before. There were very few people like Michael, she thought on a sob. How had she had the nerve to try to coddle him? Was it any wonder he'd laid into her when she practically ordered him to stay at the line shack?

They were starting up the cliff. Dusty watched with her heart in her throat. "Michael! Is there anything I can do to help?"

"Wind the slack rope around the boulder as we climb! It's tied around Lyle!"

"Yes, all right," she shouted. Glad to have something to do, Dusty ran back and forth between the anchoring boulder and the ledge. Michael had his hat pulled low on his forehead to keep the rain out of his eyes, and she wished she could see his face. Without that, his climbing looked almost effortless, and Dusty knew that he had to be exerting tremendous effort.

Lyle's bad leg was dangling, and Michael knew he had to be in a lot of pain. But the boy hung on and made no complaints. It was slow going. Michael concentrated on putting one hand over the other on the rope and securing some kind of hold for his next step. Inch by inch, minute by minute, he moved up the sheer cliff.

It seemed to last for hours, but in reality took about ten minutes. Those ten minutes were a nightmare for Dusty. She was silently weeping when the two men were finally on the upper ledge and stretched out on their backs. Michael felt the rain on his face but couldn't make his muscles move to save his soul.

Lyle seemed to be trying awfully hard to stifle a groan. Dusty knelt beside him. "Lyle, you're going to have to ride out of here."

"I know, Dusty. I can do it. Just get me up on the horse. I'll be all right once I'm up."

Dusty turned to Michael and took his hand. His eyes had been closed and he opened them to look at her. "I don't know what to say, Michael. I've never seen anything like what you did."

He smiled and squeezed her hand. "Let's get Lyle home. He needs to see a doctor."

Although his entire body felt shaky and overworked, Michael forced himself to his feet. With Dusty's help, he got Lyle up on his good leg and then virtually lifted him onto his horse. They had to ride in the same direction, as there was no room to turn the horses around on the narrow ledge.

But finally they were turned and heading out of the gorge. Lyle was slumped in his saddle, but he lifted his head at one point. "Did ya find Rhino, Mac?"

"I found him, Lyle."

"Glad to hear it. I was worried about that ornery old bull."

Michael grinned.

When the sodden caravan arrived at ranch headquarters in late afternoon, everyone rushed outside. Luke was fit to be tied. "Dusty, dammit, don't go off like that again! We—" He saw Lyle's pasty face. "What's the matter?"

"Lyle's leg is broken," Dusty said. "Someone call Bob Hanfield and ask if we can borrow his van. Lyle needs to be lying down for the trip to Casper and the hospital."

"Godalmighty," Luke muttered. "All three of you are gonna come down with pneumonia, sure as shootin'. Nancy, call Bob, will ya, honey? Jack, Wyatt, help me get Lyle down from that horse before he keels over. Dusty, you and Michael get inside and out of those wet clothes."

Dusty was too exhausted to even answer, but Luke's taking over spelled relief for her. Not that she'd headed up this little expedition, but the strain of the day had taken an enormous toll.

She made it to the house and then climbed the stairs to the second floor under her own feeble power. Her movements were slow and sluggish, she was almost too done in to shiver. In the bathroom she turned on the shower to warm up while she undressed, and then leaned against a tiled wall of the stall and let the hot water work its magic.

After drying off, she got into a nightgown and climbed into bed. Lyle was in Luke's capable hands now, and she was too tired to even think.

A light rapping on the door, followed by Nancy's voice, gave her a bit of energy. "Dusty? Are you all right?"

"Come in, Nancy."

The door opened. "Oh, good, you're in bed. You looked ready to fall down."

Dusty bunched her pillow to raise her head. "Did Bob loan us his van?"

"Sure did, glad to do it. Luke and Jack left with Lyle a few minutes ago. Poor kid. He'll be fine with medical attention, but he looked like hell."

"He had to feel like hell."

Nancy perched on the edge of the bed. "What happened out there? Luke was frantic when the storm broke and you were off God knew where. Everyone wanted to go to the rescue, but the storm was horrible. They were getting ready to start searching when the three of you rode up."

"I'm glad they waited." Dusty then related, in a quiet, drowsy tone, what had taken place, from her leading Michael to the line shack to his incredible feat with Lyle. "I've never seen anything like it, Nancy. He carried Lyle up that steep cliff on his back."

Nancy smiled softly. "He's everyone's hero today, Dusty."

"Have you talked to him?"

"No. He went to the bunkhouse and hasn't come out. Probably sleeping." Nancy got up and smoothed the blankets. "Sleep is what you need, too."

Dusty yawned. She was warm, and her bed felt as soft and caressing to her weary body as a cloud. "When Luke gets back..."

"I'll have him wake you only if there's something you should know about Lyle," Nancy said firmly.

Dusty smiled. "I guess that makes sense. See you later." Nancy left very quietly.

Twelve

Dusty slept straight through the night and awoke to sunshine. She sat up and checked the time. It was nearly eight.

Stretching, she got out of bed and went to the window. The day was glorious. Everything had a freshly bathed look and appeared brilliant in the bright sunlight.

She thought of Michael and her heart beat faster. Today was the day. She was going to initiate a discussion that would begin with an apology. *I overreacted in Florida. Please forgive me.*

Her heart and soul were tied up with Michael Crowley. Perhaps portions of her always had been. Wouldn't that account for her discontent with other men, episodes that she looked back on as mistakes? As a lack of sound judgment on her part?

She would find Michael, wherever Luke had him working, and whisk him away. Dusty laughed, low and throatily. This day was going to be hers and Michael's, and hang everything else.

Within the hour, Dusty was showered, shampooed and dressed. Hungry by then, she went down to the kitchen.

The house was unusually silent. Looking around she spotted a note on the door of the refrigerator.

Dusty,
Forgot to mention it in yesterday's mad events, but you might recall my saying something about an appointment in Casper with my hairdresser at eleven this morning. I plan to stop at the hospital and see Lyle, as well. He's fine, by the way. Has a badly broken leg, but nothing worse. Doctor wants him in the hospital for a few days because of some surgery on his leg. We notified his fiancée, and she took it well. Lyle has a very pleasant, very sensible wife in his future. See you this afternoon, probably late.

Nancy

Lyle was all right, thank God. Dusty also felt grateful that Lyle's girlfriend had been contacted.

But the very next thing that popped into her mind was that the house would be empty for most of the day, a rarity. If there was some way to get a message to Michael, she would ask him to come here.

Thoughtful, Dusty made toast and fixed herself a bowl of cold cereal. Somehow she was going to get Michael alone today. They needed to talk and...

A spiraling warmth heated her system. It wasn't only conversation she wanted from Michael, although some unreserved verbal communication was crucial.

Dusty stopped halfway to the kitchen table and let the memory of yesterday's lovemaking on that narrow little bed in the line shack overwhelm her senses. Sensation was almost in reach, close enough to make her slightly breathless.

She ate her breakfast in a speculative mood, thinking of Michael and how he might receive her apology. With all of the events of the past six weeks lined up, she felt a little silly about getting so upset in Florida. Naturally everything but his father had fled Michael's mind after an urgent call from his brother...or, at least, it seemed a lot more natural to her today than it had at the time.

At any rate, it was really a very small sin, and she wasn't going to let it bother her again.

Dusty rinsed her bowl, knife and spoon and placed them in the dishwasher. Taking the stairs to the second floor two at a time, she quickly brushed her teeth, applied lipstick and gave herself a spritz of cologne.

Then she headed downstairs and out the door. To her delight, she spotted Luke down by the barn. "Luke!" she called, and took off at a jog.

He waited for her. "How ya feeling this morning?"

"Fine. Great! Nancy left a note about Lyle. Thanks for driving him to Casper. Luke, where's Michael working today?"

"He isn't."

"He's not?" Dusty's gaze went to Michael's Bronco, which was parked in its usual spot.

Luke shook his head. "I made him take the day off."

"Then he's at the bunkhouse?"

"He was the last time I saw him."

"Um...what are you doing right now?"

"I came back to pick up a roll of barbed wire. We're replacing some wobbly fence posts. That storm did a lot of damage. Lost at least half the hay, Dusty."

"Oh...that's too bad." But Dusty's mind wasn't on flying hay and wobbly fence posts. "Luke, would you do something for me before you go?"

"Sure. What is it?"

Dusty looked him right in the eye. "Would you go to the bunkhouse and tell Michael that I'd like to see him at the house?"

A slow grin broke out on Luke's face. "Be glad to. But I'd imagine that he's pretty stiff and sore today, so you'd better take it easy on him." Luke's teasing expression sobered. "Dusty, I really hope things work out for the two of you."

"You know, I have a feeling they're going to." Smiling, she began backing away. "You're a pal. Thanks."

Luke ambled off to the bunkhouse, opened the door and went in. Michael was lying in bed but awake. He threw the blankets back and swung his feet to the floor. "Looking for me, Luke?"

"How ya feeling?"

"Lazy. Luke, I'm perfectly capable of going to work."

"Nothing doing. You earned an extra day off if any guy ever did." Luke grinned. "Anyway, Dusty wants to see you at the house."

Michael had just been thinking that he'd been a little hard on her yesterday. There'd been a lot more raw hunger than romance in their wild lovemaking, and afterward, concern about Lyle had superseded everything else.

Rising, Michael yanked on a pair of jeans. "You talked to her, apparently. Did she seem angry?" At Luke's puzzled expression, he added, "She's got good reason, if she is."

Luke rubbed his jaw. "Well, I don't think I'd exactly describe her mood as angry."

"As what, then?"

"Uh...might be best if I didn't speculate on that, Mac."

The two men's eyes met, and a silent, totally masculine exchange passed between them. Michael felt a starburst of excitement. "Got ya," he said huskily, conveying understanding. "Thanks, Luke."

Luke walked to the door. "Just so you know, Nancy's gone for the day and none of the men will be going near the house until late afternoon."

Michael cocked an eyebrow. "Nancy's gone?"

"Went to Casper. Good luck, Mac...Michael."

Whistling through his teeth, Michael went into the bathroom and turned on the shower.

Dusty changed clothes. She'd been dressed for riding, and britches and boots would not do for this meeting. Excitement mounted as she removed her bra and panties and put on a soft, loosely structured skirt and blouse with a muted pattern of blues and greens.

She touched up her makeup, brushed her hair and dabbed cologne at strategic points of her body. No jewelry. A pair of blue leather sandals, easy to kick away.

With her eyes shining like two beacons of light on a dark night, she went downstairs and directly to the kitchen window. From there the bunkhouse door was visible, and she wanted to see Michael when he came through it.

It opened. He came out. Dusty blinked. He was heading for his Bronco! Her heart nearly stopped when he crawled into it.

A few seconds later he got out of the vehicle, closed the door and started for the house.

His good looks weakened her legs. His long stride, the proud way he carried himself, nearly destroyed her ability to inhale and exhale. Her heart was hammering.

He knocked at the back door. Dusty waited a moment, put on a smile and went to let him in. "Hi."

"Hi." Michael took a good long look at her stylish but casual outfit and felt the blood start to race through his veins. She wasn't wearing a bra; the soft fabric lying on her marvelous chest was dented by two arousing bumps. "Luke said you wanted to see me."

"I do. Come in."

Now that Michael was here, Dusty felt nervous, which was just plain silly. Men didn't make her nervous.

Of course, Michael wasn't just any man. "We need to... talk," she said. *I love you.*

He nodded. "Yes, I think we do." *I love you. Do you know? Can you see it in my eyes?*

They were standing in the kitchen. "We have the whole house to ourselves. How about the living room?"

"Fine with me," Michael agreed. *A bedroom's much more versatile.*

Dusty started away but stopped abruptly. "Unless you're hungry. Have you eaten yet?"

"No, but let's talk first." *Let's do a lot of things first! Who could possibly give a damn about food right now?*

They walked to the living room, and Michael realized that he hadn't been in this room since the day of his arrival. Dusty indicated the sofa. "Please sit down."

Michael sat on one cushion, she sat on another. She lifted her chin. Nervousness was ridiculous. She was not afraid of this moment; she'd been waiting for it!

"Michael . . . the first thing I want to say is, I'm sorry."

"For what, Dusty?"

"For feeling hurt because you left Florida in such haste. It was a . . . startling morning. I kept watching for you and finally went to Cora Potter's house. I talked to the gardener."

"The gardener!" Michael frowned. "Did he know I'd gone?"

"Cora left a note on the door of the toolshed."

Michael couldn't hide his surprise. "She did? What did the gardener tell you?"

"Only that Cora and the lady who lives with her had gone away. He knew nothing about you."

"But I wasn't there and you could only conclude that I'd gone, too."

"Well, you had."

"Yes, early that morning." Michael looked at her. "You know the reason why I went."

"I eventually put it all together. Anyway, I jumped to conclusions that morning and I'm sorry."

Michael leaned forward. "But, deep down, what do you really think of a man who could make love to a woman at night and forget her in the morning?"

Dusty stiffened slightly. "I've been trying not to think of it in that context."

"Yet you have."

"I did . . . at first."

Michael inched a little closer. "That's why you hung up on me, and that's what was in your mind when I showed up without warning."

"Yes," she whispered.

Michael laid his hand on her thigh. "You said that was the first thing you wanted to say. Was there something else?"

Dusty was looking at the big, decidedly masculine hand on her skirt. She could smell Michael and feel him, and her heart was doing loop-the-loops in her chest.

She cleared her throat. "I was wrong about your...career move. You have every right to do what you want with your life, and you're a...very good cowhand." Her eyes closed briefly, a moment stolen for self-castigation. "You're more than a good cowhand. You're courageous and capable and..."

"And?" Michael prompted softly.

Dusty tried, but she couldn't get it out. Although close to bursting with the emotion, she could not say "I love you" without some sign from him that he felt the same.

"And you have a job here for as long as you want," she finished lamely.

"Ah, a job." Michael moved his hand ever so slightly, a barely perceptible caress. He looked into her eyes and saw permission, even an invitation to be bolder. He adored that special glow in her eyes and savored the expectation in the air, the anticipation. She had more to say, just as he did.

It would all come out today, her feelings, his. He'd been waiting for this moment, since Florida, really, although once in Wyoming he hadn't been able to estimate timing.

Lowering his head, he pressed a tender kiss to a corner of Dusty's mouth. She shivered at the delicious assault of her senses, and said, "We...seem to affect each other...very strongly."

"Very strongly," he whispered, and kissed the other corner of her lips. His hand moved on her skirt, working it upward. "What do you suppose it means?"

Dusty was getting dizzy. With her eyes closed, her head swayed in a slow rhythm, a sensual movement in tune with his soft kisses to her cheeks, her forehead, her chin.

"You mentioned...commitment," she said in a husky voice.

"No, *you* mentioned commitment. I said I wanted the whole ball of wax. If we played again."

"We...did play." Michael's hand was under her skirt and on her bare thigh. "And we would have again...in the rain...if we'd been...alone."

Michael nibbled at her ear. "Are we going to play today?"

Dusty's spirit soared. How she wanted him! Until the end of time! How could she have been such a fool to risk losing him?

She opened her eyes. "Move your hand a little higher."

He did, slowly, and encountered lush female flesh instead of underwear. His eyes darkened. "This isn't a game anymore. Dusty, I love you. I love you and want you, not just for today. For the rest of our lives."

Tears filled her eyes. Speech eluded her for a breathless few seconds. It came back in a rush of emotion. "Oh, Michael!" She threw her arms around his neck. "I love you, too. I've been dying to say so."

They clung to each other. "When did you know?" Dusty whispered.

"Sixteen years ago." Michael couldn't touch her enough. His lips roamed her face and hair, his hands traveled her back and breasts and legs. He was under her skirt, then over it. He nuzzled her throat and kissed her teary eyes and beautiful mouth. "And last February. The minute I saw you on that beach. I knew you instinctively, I guess, even though it took me a day to really believe it."

He pulled her head back to see her face. "Why are you crying?"

"Because I wish there'd never been anyone else, no other man. We should never have been torn apart."

"It happened, Dusty, we can't go back. There were other women...my wife. She was important, I can't say she wasn't."

"Don't talk about it, not just yet." Dusty kissed his lips. "Love me...just love me."

"I do, baby, I love you." Michael pushed her down on the sofa and laid over her. "In the mud, on a couch, it doesn't matter, does it? You've made me come alive, Dusty. That's what you've done for me, brought me back to life. You and Wyoming."

His kisses became hot and demanding but always pleasuring, lifting Dusty onto a sensual plane where nothing else had meaning. She kissed and caressed him, whispering over and over again, "I love you . . . I love you," until it became a soft chant of utter emotion.

Neither mentioned protection. Dusty's skirt was bunched at her hips, Michael's jeans and undershorts had been pushed down and out of the way. They made love greedily, as hungrily as they had yesterday.

Yet there was something profound and eternal about it, an element that hadn't been present in the line shack. It was love admitted, love returned, love shared, and it bound them more tightly than mere lust ever could.

And then, only because of a vague glance beyond the man in her arms, Dusty remembered where they were.

The living room. If Nancy should return earlier than she'd planned . . . if Luke should suddenly need something from the house . . .

"Michael, we have to go upstairs," she whispered raggedly. He looked as dazed as she felt. They were in the throes of passion, intimately joined.

"Now?"

"Yes . . . now."

He moved his hips and slid deeper into her heat. "I don't know if I can."

Her lips parted for a breath of air. "We have to. Someone could walk in on us." Michael groaned. "Besides, my love," she whispered. "We can completely undress upstairs and share a huge bed."

That picture got Michael's attention. Still, it was painful to leave her at that precise moment. He struggled to his feet, but then got an unrestricted view of her body. Kneeling beside the sofa, he kissed the soft, sensitive skin of her abdomen.

"Upstairs," Dusty reminded, afraid of getting lost in the sweet torment of his mouth on secret places.

Michael gave a shaky laugh and got up again. This time he yanked up his jeans and helped Dusty to her feet. Her skirt fell into place. He hauled her to him and kissed her mouth, growling, "That bed seems a long way off."

"It's just a short walk." She tried to smile. "If our faces weren't so flushed, we'd look almost normal." With her arm around his waist, Dusty urged him from the room.

"Anyone looking at us now would know exactly what we were doing." In the hall, Michael moved her against the wall and lifted her skirt. "They'd know now, for sure," he whispered, sliding into her again.

If Dusty hadn't been trying desperately to maintain some small hold on sensibility, she would have completely forgotten the trip up the stairs. "Michael . . . please . . ."

He was an impatient lover, which didn't displease Dusty; she, too, was hot-blooded.

But never like this.

After two more stops to kiss and touch along the way, they finally made it to Dusty's bedroom. She shut the door.

They were disheveled, both of them, hair and clothing awry. Dusty's downstairs inhibitions had vanished when the door closed. This room was hers alone, no one would come walking in on them, not if every person she knew should suddenly congregate on the first floor of the house.

"Now," she said low and deliberately provocative. "I'm yours." A slow-burning smile appeared on Michael's lips. Dusty grinned wickedly. "Damn, you're handsome!"

Laughing, they collided and fell to the bed. Elation was in their kisses. Happiness. Lightheartedness. Qualities they hadn't experienced with each other. Laughter felt wonderful, and they rolled over and over on the bed, wrapped together, being silly together.

Then they were serious again, another facet had been added to their feelings, the wonder of laughing together.

Leaning over Dusty, Michael smoothed back the silky hair from her forehead. "You're beautiful, so beautiful."

She touched his face, his mouth. "Is this a dream? Michael, how did we both happen to be in Florida at the same time after so many years?"

He kissed her fingertips. "We'll never know." His lips moved to hers, and a sweet kiss rapidly evolved to one of need. They lavished love on each other. Dusty wriggled free of his weight and sat up to remove her blouse. Michael lay there and watched, his eyes heavy and smoky with adoration and desire.

She slipped out of her skirt and reached for the buttons on his shirt. "Don't move," she whispered. "I want to undress you."

"Might be hard to do if I don't move," Michael drawled.

"Only move when I tell you to."

They laughed about this, too, her trying to get him out of his clothes with a minimum of movement, especially when he couldn't leave her be. His hands teased her breasts, toyed sassily with her behind, swooped down her legs to tickle behind her knees.

Finally, though, he was lying there without a stitch of clothing. Dusty started at his eyes and worked her gaze downward, slowly, sensually. The return trip was every bit as drawn out. "Damn, you're handsome," she said again, her voice husky, the phrase rife with sin and seduction.

"Come 'ere," he growled, and pulled her down on top of him. Their kisses were without playfulness, this time there would be no interruptions. His hands heated the skin of her back and hips. She rubbed her breasts against his chest and felt his responsive shudders.

Michael rolled them over, placing Dusty on her back. He twisted to capture a rosy, erect nipple with his mouth and brought both him and Dusty closer to the brink with gentle sucking. Her legs were open for him, and he skimmed a hand down her belly to the hot, moist nest of her femaleness.

Soft moans spilled from Dusty's lips. Her love for this man was all-consuming, increasing her passion for him a hundredfold. There was, for her, not another man on earth like Michael. He was unique... and hers.

The knowledge swelled within her, dazzling her mind, sensitizing her body. She urged his head up for a kiss, and lavished his mouth with her love. His penetration was swift and heady, drawing a groan of intense pleasure from her throat.

They looked into each other's eyes. "I want this perfect for you," Michael whispered.

She was trembling. "It is, it couldn't be more perfect." Her hips rose, drawing him deeper, taking him farther. His eyelids drooped, making his eyes hot and heavy-looking. She felt emotion crawl into her throat and tighten it. With Michael, she always got teary.

He withdrew and advanced, going slowly. "It is perfect. You're perfect."

Her smile was misty. Desire was rampant in her body, but so was love, the feeling that she'd seen between a few elderly couples in her life, where even at seventy, eighty, they still touched... and smiled... and spoke kindly to each other.

Squeezing Michael to herself in a rush of emotion, she whispered, "I will love you until the day I die."

Caresses and movements roughened. Dusty's nails bit into Michael's back. Emotions electrified. Desires exploded.

Their completion was cataclysmic, a torrent of gasps and movements that dazed and amazed the both of them.

Replete and drained, they lay nearly lifeless. Dusty didn't care if she ever got off this bed again. There was nothing, not anywhere, that she would rather be doing than lying beneath Michael and drifting in her own consciousness. If she suggested it, would he consent to lying thusly for the rest of their lives?

Appreciating the nonsensical turn of her thoughts, Dusty smiled, a mere twitching of her lips. Michael stirred, lifted his head lazily and looked at her. The flames that had burned so wildly in his eyes were subdued and banked.

"We have plans to make," he said softly.

Dusty's smile widened. "Yes, we do."

His expression became teasing. "Can we eat first?"

She laughed. "You're hungry."

"Starving. Do you think there's anything in the refrigerator?"

"There's always something in the refrigerator in this house. Nancy sees to that. Do you want to go downstairs, or should I bring something up?"

Michael looked pleased. "You'd do that?"

"For you, anything. Just name it."

Dusty had spoken lightly, but Michael didn't take it that way. "You mean it, don't you?"

Her hands traveled up his arms to his shoulders. "I mean it." She looked at him and felt a developing breathlessness. "If you want food, you'd better let me up. Otherwise . . ."

Michael grinned. "An insatiable woman? How'd I get so lucky?"

Dusty sobered. "How'd we *both* get so lucky?" Her mood switched again. "Move, buster! I'm ready to cook, and if you miss this urge, you might not eat until tonight!"

Thirteen

They were sitting on the bed, picking at the remains of a lettuce-and-tomato salad, cold chicken and blueberry muffins. They'd talked while eating. Michael had briefly and very sweetly, Dusty thought, discussed his wife. In turn, Dusty had given him the pertinent facts of her marriage to Trent. They had touched on Tom, Michael's brother, and Tom's disapproval of Michael's decision to leave New York. Yesterday had been rehashed, particularly Michael's rescue of Lyle.

"I misjudged you so badly," Dusty said on a rueful sigh. "Can you believe that I was even angry because you hadn't tried to contact me after you were sent back to New York sixteen years ago?" She shook her head, finding it hard to believe herself.

Michael looked stunned. "Dusty...I tried every way possible to contact you. I wrote..."

"You wrote? Michael, *I* wrote."

It was abundantly clear what had happened. Their parents had intercepted their mail, their telephone calls, every attempt to communicate.

At Dusty's shattered expression, Michael said soothingly, "They did what they thought was right, honey. We were too young for marriage."

"I know," Dusty groaned. "But, my Lord... so many wasted years." She quickly picked up the remnants of their meal, got off the bed and put everything on the tray she'd used to carry it upstairs. She was wearing a robe, having braved that state of undress to get their lunch together.

Michael got up, too, and went into the bathroom. Dusty pulled the blankets around to straighten the bed. It was awful, she thought, how the past could weight the present. The Crowleys and the Tremaynes had believed in what they'd done for their children, and from a practical standpoint, Dusty couldn't fault their motives. But there *had* been a lot of wasted years, and maybe their premature marriage would have been a success.

One thing she knew for certain: If Michael had been in the picture, she wouldn't have squandered her adulthood in searching for the right man!

He came back wearing a towel. They met in the middle of the room and kissed tenderly, their embrace signifying a communion that was both old and new.

"Dusty, do you trust me now? I mean, really trust me?"

"Of course I do."

"What about that morning in Florida?"

Dusty slipped from his arms. "You had to leave."

"Yes, but you didn't know that. Honey, I can see the whole thing. You, waiting for me to show up. Your tension growing, your nerves getting raw. If it had been me left behind without an explanation, I would have been hurt, too."

"I was... hurt." Dusty put on a smile. "But it's in the past, Michael. I'd really rather not talk about it. You had to leave, you had no choice."

"But I could have left you a message. Cora managed one for her gardener."

Dusty stared at him. "What do you want me to say, Michael? You had to go. You were probably in a panic over your father."

"Yes, I felt some panic. But I didn't forget you, Dusty. I want to prove it to you."

"Well, that's just not possible to do, is it? Michael, I've come to terms with it. Please don't worry about it."

Michael went to her and drew her into his arms. He spoke with his face in her hair. "The first day I got here, I knew how deep the hurting went. You hated me."

"No!" Dusty pushed away from him. "Michael, I didn't hate you. I was angry, yes, but when you told me about your father dying, and then, the next day, about Tom calling that morning . . . Michael, I never hated you."

Extending his hand, Michael touched her chest with his forefinger. "There's a little pocket of hurt still left in there, isn't there?"

Dusty frowned. "You sound like you *want* it to be there. I don't understand where this is leading."

Michael became deadly serious. "I *don't* want it there. I want it gone, and there's only one way to eliminate it. Proof."

Dusty sucked in a breath. "I have no idea what you're talking about. I'm not looking for proof, and you're making me very upset." She watched, uneasily, while Michael discarded the towel and pulled on his jeans. "What are you doing?"

"I've something to ask you."

"Yes?" She knew she sounded suspicious, but this conversation and Michael getting dressed were making her uncomfortable.

Michael dug into the right-hand pocket of his jeans and walked over to her. He put his hands on her hair. "Dusty, will you marry me?"

The breath whooshed out of her. "My Lord! You scared me to death for a minute." She threw her arms around him. "Yes, I'll marry you. Oh, Michael, yes, yes, yes!"

"Then take this."

She stepped back. He took her left hand and slid a diamond ring on her finger. "I bought it in New York," he said quietly. "It was in the Bronco."

Dusty looked at the beautiful ring and then at him with stars in her eyes. "You bought it before you came to Wyoming?"

He nodded.

"Oh, Michael," she whispered, expecting to be scooped into his arms.

Instead he put on his shirt and questioned, "Do you remember that book I asked you about? The one you had with you in Florida?"

Confusion flooded Dusty. "Why are you bringing that up now? And don't waste your breath trying to convince me that you've got a sudden yen to read a historical romance! Michael, this is crazy. You've just asked me to marry you!"

Tucking the tails of his shirt into his jeans, Michael came closer. "I know, but this is important. Concentrate, Dusty. What did you do with that book?"

Dusty rolled her eyes. "I don't believe this."

He took her by the shoulders. "Didn't you say you'd do anything for me?"

"Yes! And I meant it! But why in hell are we talking about a book?"

"Because it's important!"

For the first time, Dusty really thought about that book. Yes, she remembered it now. It had been on the table on the terrace. She'd almost left it behind. And Michael was glowering at her right now because of it, because of a stupid, damned book that...

She froze as a glimpse of what might have happened struck her. "Why is it so important, Michael?"

"You're catching on, aren't you?"

"Maybe."

"What did you do with the book, Dusty?"

"I...don't know."

"But you don't throw books away."

"No...never."

"It's in the house, somewhere."

"It could be." Springing to life, Dusty went to her closet. "There's usually a few books in here." With Michael right on her heels, she pawed through half a dozen paperbacks on a shelf. "No, it isn't here."

She dashed to the bed stand and yanked open its two drawers. "Not here, either." Dusty straightened her back. "Wait a minute. I almost left it in Florida because it wasn't very good. The reason I didn't was because of a bedridden friend. Michael, Nancy took a box of books over to Louise Myers a few weeks ago. I'll bet that book was in the box."

Michael wiped his mouth in a perturbed gesture. "Can you call Louise and find out?"

"Yes. Her number's in my directory in the office. Wait here. I'll run down and get it. Only take a minute."

While Dusty was gone, Michael went to the closet and checked the paperbacks on the shelf again. None of them was red, none had a bookmark.

He had to wonder why proof seemed so critical now. He and Dusty were committed, she was wearing his ring. There was very little with the power to alter their present status.

But he kept thinking of Dusty that morning, waiting, worrying, learning from a total stranger that he'd left Florida, and ultimately thinking the worst. He thought of what she'd told him about her mistakes with men. She was an honest, forthright woman and deserved the same courtesy from men.

His deeply rooted attitude was, he finally recognized, no more than what he'd told her while they were making love: He wanted it perfect for her, and if he could eradicate that one small pocket of dissension in their relationship, it *would* be perfect.

Dusty rushed in and waved a piece of paper. "I've got the number. I'll call Louise now." Sitting on the bed, she picked up the phone and punched out a number.

Michael sat down beside her. "Jill? This is Dusty Tremayne. Would it be possible to speak to your mother?

Thanks." Dusty put her hand over the mouthpiece. "Louise lives with her daughter."

"Hello?" she heard.

"Louise? This is Dusty Tremayne. How are you?"

"I'm fine, Dusty. How are you, honey?"

"I'm fine, too, Louise."

Michael listened through a few minutes of small talk before Dusty got to the point. "Louise, Nancy brought you a box of books about ten days, two weeks ago. Have you read them?"

"Not yet, honey. Everyone is so generous with reading material that I've got several boxes ahead. Why, Dusty?"

"Um . . . Louise, is the box handy?"

"I can have Jill bring it to me, if you'd like."

"Could you, please? I hate being a bother, but . . ."

"No bother at all. Jill! Jill, honey, would you come in here and bring me that box of books in the corner?"

Dusty heard murmured phrases and muffled noises through the phone. "Her daughter is bringing her the box," she told Michael. She switched the phone to her other hand and looked at her beautiful ring, then gave Michael a warm smile.

"All right, Dusty, I have it."

Dusty drew a breath. "Louise, look through it and tell me if there's a book with a very bright red cover."

"All right. Hmm, this one looks good, and here's one I've been wanting to read. The author was on a talk show just the other day. Oh, here's a red one, *Pearls of Passion*. Is that the one, Dusty?"

"That's it. Hold on a second, Louise." Dusty covered the mouthpiece. "She's got it, Michael. Now what?"

"Ask her to look for a bookmark."

Dusty cleared her throat. "Louise, is there a bookmark in *Pearls of Passion*?"

"Well, let me see. Why, yes, there is. Very pretty one, too."

Dusty had been looking at Michael. "There's a bookmark," she whispered, and could hardly believe it when he flopped back on the bed and shouted, "Thank you, God!"

Michael popped up again. "Ask her to read the handwriting on it, out loud."

It was all very clear now. Dusty didn't know whether to kiss or sock Michael. "You could have told me," she hissed at him before requesting sweetly into the phone, "There should be some handwriting on the bookmark, Louise. Would you read what it says to me, please?"

"Of course, dear. Oh, I see it. Very small writing. It says, 'Dusty.' My goodness, is this a note to you?"

"I believe it is, Louise."

Louise began. "'Dusty, My father's had a heart attack. Am flying home at once. My telephone number is 555-9878. Call me. All my love, Michael.' Well, my goodness," Louise murmured. "Was that what you wanted to hear, honey?"

"Yes, Louise, thank you. The book is unimportant, but would you save the bookmark for me?"

"I certainly will."

Dusty put the phone down and gave Michael a long, silent look. His grin wasn't at all soothing. "How could you do such a thing?" she finally got out, and stood up to flounce around the room. "I can't believe it. I went through hell, and all this time, that damned bookmark was right under my nose!"

Michael was leaning back on his elbows, and he couldn't stop grinning. "I thought you'd see it right away. I looked for something to write on and there wasn't anything, not even a newspaper."

Dusty stopped and glared. "Well, you don't have to look so smug about it! I don't find this particularly amusing."

"You've got a temper, haven't you?"

"I never used to have!"

"Maybe I bring out the worst side of you."

Hesitating only a moment, Dusty ran and jumped right on the middle of him. He yelped then laughed, and he easily tipped her over and held her down. "Wanna play rough, huh, sweetheart?"

"You deserve to die," Dusty fumed. "You could have told me."

"No, I couldn't. I thought about it, but you weren't only mad at me, Dusty, you'd crossed me off."

"Let me up."

"No way." Michael had straddled her and was holding her hands over her head. "Tell me you love me." Haughtily Dusty turned her face away. Michael dipped his head and whispered in her ear, "Tell me you want my body, baby."

Dusty ignored the thrills zapping her senses. "All this time you let me walk around with a wounded air. You knew you'd written that note, and you let me suffer and..."

"I let you heal," Michael murmured, his breath on her ear creating tingles on her skin. "You loved me in spite of it all, you agreed to marry me, and you love me now. Say it."

"Every time we saw each other... when I rode out to the cows' pasture and you were working..., at meals... yesterday... talking about the 'whole ball of wax'... and taking advantage of my weakness for you... and rescuing Lyle... through it all, you knew."

"Have you got a weakness for me, honey? Tell me about it."

"I'm... mad at you."

"You're mad *for* me." Michael kneed her legs apart and rubbed his body against her most sensitive spot.

"You're squashing me."

He chuckled. "If I let go of your hands, what will you do?"

"Scratch out your eyes."

"In that case..." Michael transferred both of her hands to his left and brought his right down. He moved aside enough to untie the sash of her robe.

Dusty squirmed a little, *only* a little. "You are not going to have your way with me."

"No? You're not going to cooperate? Or enjoy it even a tiny bit?" With the panels of the robe separated, he began to fondle her breasts. His hand moved slowly, tantalizing her nipples into rigidity, cupping the ripe fullness of her bosom. He saw her eyes close and her mouth open slightly, the tip of her tongue flick as she moistened her lips.

He put his face very close to hers. "Put that sweet little tongue in my mouth. Make me crazy from wanting you."

Her eyes fluttered open. "You're already crazy," she whispered.

"Crazy about you."

"I've never known anyone like you."

"Ditto, sweetheart."

Dusty inhaled slowly. Michael watched her chest expand and grinned. "Do that again."

"You're wicked."

"I'm in love."

She gave up all pretense. "So am I. Oh, Michael, so am I."

Pretense vanished from Michael's face, as well. "I'm sorry it hit you so hard. I wasn't sure we'd ever find the bookmark, and I was afraid you'd think I'd made it up." He released her hands and kissed her lips. "Tell me you love me."

Her arms slid around his neck. "I love you."

"Never stop staying it."

Dusty thought of Trent, who'd grown to resent those words very quickly. But she relegated him and every other man she'd ever known to the trash bin, which was where they belonged. "I won't, my love, not ever."

Michael smiled at her. "Now tell me you want my body."

"I want your body. Naked. On mine. In mine." She then looked exaggeratedly puzzled, which prompted a question from Michael as to what she was thinking. "I'm trying to figure out if I'm more in love with your mind or your body."

He threw back his head and laughed, uproariously.

Epilogue

We cannot leave Dusty and Michael just yet. This is what happened to them.

They had a huge wedding. Cora Potter and Mary Tanaka came to Wyoming for the big doings. Tom Crowley and his wife did not, although they sent an expensive set of crystal stemware and a lukewarm note of congratulations.

Michael told Dusty not to feel slighted. "We'll fix old Tom, honey. One of these days we'll drop in on him, and when he meets you he'll understand everything."

So, obviously, Michael was planning a trip to New York for some time in the future. That was fine with Dusty. For that matter, anything Michael did was fine with her.

Almost anything, she found out.

On their wedding night she presented Michael with an envelope. "Open it," she requested when he merely looked at it strangely.

He did so slowly and extracted a legal document, which he read in quiet amazement. "You gave me half interest in the ranch."

Dusty was radiant with happiness. "It's my wedding gift to you, my wonderful, precious darling."

He nodded, hesitated briefly and smiled. "This is . . . astounding. Thank-you hardly seems adequate."

She laughed a tinkling joyous laugh. "Thank-you is very adequate."

Michael thought for a moment, then smiled again. "My gift was held up, but you'll receive it in due time."

She did, although by the time her bank statement arrived three weeks later, she'd nearly forgotten about it. Actually, the bank statement lay on the desk in her office for four days before she got around to opening it. There were so many more interesting and marvelous things to do these days than balancing a bank statement.

For one thing, she and Michael had decided to build a new house on the ranch. Luke and Nancy weren't going anywhere, and as roomy as the old Tremayne house was, it wasn't big enough for two couples. Michael was so impulsive with lovemaking, Dusty was pleased to discover, not completely content to confine their physical affection to the bedroom. As in love as she was, she hated sidestepping her husband's sexual advances and could hardly wait until they were living by themselves.

At any rate, she decided one afternoon to catch up on the bookwork and allotted a reconciliation of her bank account as her first task.

Her bank balance staggered her. Frowning, she studied the information on the statement and saw an enormous deposit, which she certainly hadn't made. At first she thought the bank had made a dreadful error. She reached for the phone to call the institution, but the date of the deposit suddenly leaped out at her.

Instantly she knew the score. Michael had made that deposit! This was his gift!

Fury racked her, because it wasn't a gift at all. He'd paid her for the fifty-percent interest in the ranch she'd given him on their wedding night!

Dusty waited until they'd retired for the night before saying anything, but she'd been cool throughout supper and Michael knew it.

In their bedroom, he pulled her close and kissed her lips. "Ready to tell me what's bothering you?"

Dusty stayed in his arms, but she wasn't exactly cooperative. "Money."

"You got the bank statement."

She tipped her head back to see his face. "Just tell me why. I gave you a gift, not a contract of sale."

Michael dropped his hands and walked away. "It was too much."

"Your *deposit* was too much! Aren't we partners? How are you looking at this marriage?"

"As permanent," he said flatly. "But I'm not taking the ranch as a gift."

"Why didn't you say so when I gave you the new deed?"

"It was our wedding night. I didn't want an argument." Michael looked at her. "I don't want one now, either." His eyes narrowed. "It's not open for debate."

"Oh, it's not. You threw my gift in my face!"

"Give me some cuff links ... or a horse ... or a car ... or even some shaving cream, but you're not *giving* me half of a ranch that's been in your family for generations!"

"I never offered it to another man."

Michael sighed. "Dusty, I know you see what you did as generous and based on love." He shook his head. "I'm sorry, but I can't take it. The money in your account is yours. If you want the fifty percent put back in your name, I'll take back the money."

"You're stubborn and ... and awful!"

He came to her and took her hands. His eyes were burning. "What I am is a cowhand. Do you think I could run this ranch? Not on your life! Luke can ... and does. You can ... and do. In time I'll learn the fundamentals, count on it. But it won't be for a while, and if you can't deal with that, God help us."

They went to bed and didn't make love. It was their first cool night together. Michael turned his back in one direction, Dusty turned her back in the other, and the space in between them was wide enough for a third person.

Michael went to work in the morning and Dusty paced away the day. She couldn't talk to Nancy about it, not when the very foundation of her marriage seemed to be crumbling.

That afternoon, Cora Potter called, surprising Dusty. "How are you, dear?"

"Fine, Cora. And you?"

"I've been thinking of Michael. Is he all right?"

Dusty laughed shakily. "Yes . . . of course. He's working right now, but I could have him call you this evening."

"No, no, I'll talk to you. It's amazing how he's taken to ranch life, isn't it?"

"Amazing," Dusty agreed dryly.

"You don't mind him giving up his law career, do you?"

"I'm not sure I completely understand his decision, Cora, but no, I don't mind."

"That's good to hear. I have a special affection for Michael. He's always reminded me of my own son."

"I didn't know you had a son, Cora."

"He died in Korea, Dusty. He was a marvelous person, bright, intelligent, handsome, and with the most wonderful sense of humor."

"Oh, Cora, I'm so sorry."

"Yes, well, thousands of wonderful young men died, didn't they? I took it very hard, I must admit. I blamed his father, you know. George had encouraged his participation in the war, loyalty to country, protecting the American way, all that sort of thing. I don't think women feel quite the same about their sons going off to war as men do.

"Of course, that all passed. But I was a very unhappy lady for quite a long while. Even left George for eight months, or rather, George booted me out. Made his life miserable. Men do have their pride, although the trait appears more like stubbornness at times."

"Stubbornness," Dusty repeated quietly. "Yes, I know what you mean."

Cora chuckled. "Yes, I'm sure you do. Dusty, give Michael my best. And dear, take heart. I can tell by your voice that everything isn't a hundred percent. Give it time . . . and patience."

Dusty put the phone down and thought about life and death and pride . . . and Michael. Her beloved Michael. He'd done nothing but be the man she had once prayed to meet. Yes, he had pride, and thank God for that.

So, Michael and Dusty's final relationship didn't begin until that night. Michael was so glad that Dusty was smiling instead of scowling during dinner, he whisked her up the stairs and into their bedroom the minute the meal was over.

They hugged and kissed with an almost frantic renewal of their feelings for each other. They brought those feelings to bed and made incredible beautiful love, and when their physical desire was satisfied, they talked.

"I love you just the way you are," Dusty told him. "Don't ever change."

Michael laughed softly. "We'll change as we get older, sweetheart, both of us. But change doesn't necessitate a loss of affection."

"Michael, I want a baby."

He tipped her chin. "I'll be more than happy to contribute to that goal. Shall we start now?"

"Now? We just . . ."

"Now, Dusty."

"Yes, my love," she whispered. "Oh, yes!"

* * * * *

SILHOUETTE® Desire®

MYSTERY MATES!

**Six sexy Bachelors explosively pair with
six sultry Bachelorettes to find the Valentine's
surprise of a lifetime.**

Get to know the mysterious men who breeze into the lives of these
unsuspecting women. Slowly uncover—as the heroines themselves
must do—the missing pieces of the puzzle that add up to hot, *hot*
heroes! You begin by knowing nothing about these enigmatic men,
but soon you'll know *everything*. . . .

Heat up your winter with:

#763   THE COWBOY by Cait London

#764   THE STRANGER by Ryanne Corey

#765   THE RESCUER by Peggy Moreland

#766   THE WANDERER by Beverly Barton

#767   THE COP by Karen Leabo

#768   THE BACHELOR by Raye Morgan

Mystery Mates—coming in February from Silhouette Desire.
Because you never know who you'll meet. . . .

Silhouette Books
is proud to present
our best authors,
their best books...
and the best in
your reading pleasure!

Throughout 1993, look for exciting books
by these top names in contemporary
romance:

CATHERINE COULTER—
Af-tershocks in February

FERN MICHAELS—
Whisper My Name in March

DIANA PALMER—
Heather's Song in March

ELIZABETH LOWELL—
Love Song for a Raven in April

SANDRA BROWN
(previously published under
the pseudonym Erin St. Claire)—
Led Astray in April

LINDA HOWARD—
All That Glitters in May

When it comes to passion,
we wrote the book.

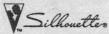

BOBT1R

For all those readers who've been looking for something a little bit different, a little bit spooky, let Silhouette Books take you on a journey to the dark side of love with

If you like your romance mixed with a hint of danger, a taste of something eerie and wild, you'll love Shadows. This new line will send a shiver down your spine and make your heart beat faster. It's full of romance and more—and some of your favorite authors will be featured right from the start. Look for our four launch titles wherever books are sold, because you won't want to miss a single one.

THE LAST CAVALIER—Heather Graham Pozzessere
WHO IS DEBORAH?—Elise Title
STRANGER IN THE MIST—Lee Karr
SWAMP SECRETS—Carla Cassidy

After that, look for two books every month, and prepare to tremble with fear—and passion.

SILHOUETTE SHADOWS, coming your way in March.

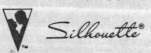

SHAD1